Maggot Girl

Episode 3: Denouement of Depravity

Otis Bateman

Copyright © 2022 by Otis Bateman.

All rights reserved.

No portion of this book may be reproduced in any form without written permission from the publisher or author, except as permitted by U.S. copyright law.

Edited by 360 Editing (a division of Uncomfortably Dark Horror).

Contents

Dedication	V
	VI
1. Fuck The Pain Away	1
2. Desperately Seeking Morticia	6
3. Kim Cleans Up	8
4. Choices, Or Lack Therof	14
5. Premonitions Of War	19
6. Making My Way Back To You	22
7. Bringing A Knife To A Gunfight	23
8. Roll That Flashback Footage	32
9. Losing Lurch	40
10. Become Wrath	46
11. Kim Deals Damage	50
12. Judith To The Rescue	55
13. Homing In	59
14. Follow The Bloody Breadcrumbs	60
15. Heaven's Biggest Angel	69

16.	Homing In Part 2	74
17.	Crushing The Little Piggy	75
18.	Momma Bear	80
19.	The GoodFather	85
20.	Batter Up	90
21.	The Incest Chapter	97
22.	Scissor Me Timbers	103
23.	Molesting The Cadaver	109
24.	Deus Ex Machina, Bitches	117
25.	A Felched Finale	122
26.	A Family Reunited	133
27.	Happily, Ever After?	139
28.	A New Beginning	143
Afterword		147

Dedicated to Aron Beauregard and Judith Sonnet. You both have been a limitless source of inspiration for me. Your kindness, undying work ethic, and unselfish nature have been greatly appreciated. Thank you for pushing me to be a better writer than I ever imagined possible.
<3

"Writing Is The One Art Form That Really Should Allow You To Hang Yourself."—Peter Sotos, Void Books Interview

Chapter One

Fuck The Pain Away

I QUICKLY STRIDE TO my quarters in a complete mental quandary, my mind racing at an accelerated pace, as I try to figure out a way to physically unfuck the situation that Lurch and I have found ourselves drowning in. Why couldn't Pat Bale just have left us alone and done his fucking job? He had his pick when it came to getting poontang. Why on God's green earth would he want me???

Nope, he had to be a fuck boy and try to rape and kill me. Luckily for this gore gal, I have a musclebound behemoth as my guardian angel. Of course, he had to die, and together we made it happen, brutally, but now what? The minute Lux surveys the CAM footage of the compound and sees what we did to his grisly golden boy, Lurch and I are toast. He could already be on his way to the Hurt 2 The Core compound as I speak to put an array of bullets in our fucking heads! FUCK MY LIFE!!!!!!

I shooed Lurch off to bed so I can figure out a solution to the quicksand that we find ourselves sinking in. Thank

God he has a simple mind. I just checked in on the big goon and bless his heart, he is sawing logs in dreamland like he does not have a care in the world. I give him a kiss on his globular head and stare down at his sleeping form. How can I keep us both safe when the shit hits the proverbial fan in the morning? All this worry is giving my brain a massive headache. I need to alleviate it, even if it is only for a little while. I go into my room and plop heavily on my bed with an exhausted sigh.

"Fuck me gently with a chainsaw!" I shriek into my pillow like a teen girl throwing a tantrum over being jilted by a boy.

I scan the room looking for something, anything to give my tired noggin a brief respite, and then I see it like a *Where's Waldo* puzzle peeking out behind my trash can. It is what is left of a partially eaten meatball sub sandwich with extra jalapenos that I was munching on the other day from Mr. Goodcents. Only now it is being devoured by a swarm of hungry maggots. Their writhing mass hypnotizes me almost immediately. I vaguely feel drool spill down the side of my lip as my brain almost instantly decides what to do; I want it all stuffed inside of me to momentarily quell this debilitating anxiety that is clutching my heart in a death grip.

My cunt is already gushing in anticipation for what comes next. I had not debased myself in years. I have tried so hard to stay on the straight and narrow when it came to filling my poon with poison, but right now, I need a release from all this worry. I want to drown myself in debauchery and lewdness. Maybe afterwards, it will get my mind right so I can figure out what to do. I am Jack's dark carnal desires reawakened.

I bring the flyblown sandwich over to where I am sitting, and gaze at it like I am transfixed by its magnificence. The hoagie has taken on a teal hue, as it has molded heavily. I catch the few maggots that fall from the meal and place them back on the sub. I remove every stitch of clothing and lay the pile of neatly folded garments onto my bed, and then sit Indian style on the floor nude, as I pinched my hardened nipples and knead my aching breasts. My hands slowly and lithely glide down my body, towards my glistening wet honey pot. The heat emanating from my sex is on a whole other level. I knew this was what I needed to soothe the savage beast. Why was I so reluctant to debase myself? This is who I am, after all, nothing more than a human septic tank meant to be encased with filth.

My fingers nimbly part my lips as I use a thumb to massage my blood engorged clitoris. My body spasms from the immediate sensations, and I bite my lower lip to quell a guttural moan from escaping.

As I vigorously frig my aching cunny, I stare at the sub sandwich in famished anticipation. I watch the countless maggots feast and swirl upon the rotting and festering meatball's, its fetid, pungent stench only causes me to masturbate at a more frenzied, animalistic state. My pussy is throbbing in anticipation as I cup the sandwich in my free hand, while gaping open my ravenous cunt with the other. In one fell swoop, I plunge the malodorous meal into my yawning, gaping sex. A smattering of my baby's plummet to the ground and fall around my taint and puckered asshole. They playfully wriggle against my brown eye, causing me to squirt and ejaculate into their squirming forms.

With my free hand, I collect them and deposit them into my frothing axe wound, as a massive orgasm wracks my body to its limit in terms of pleasure. My pussy literary begins coming like a man's cock. Thick ropes of jism, intermingled with a speckling of maggots, spurt out of my larvae encased cunt. My mind is reeling from the sick pleasure of debasing myself like I did in the old days. I never want to go back normality ever again for as long as I live.

It stretched my sex to its capacity, much like a suitcase filled beyond its capabilities, and now it will not latch no matter how much you struggle with it. I feel like I am bursting, pregnant with pestilence. I use a compact to look at my drooling sex. A smattering of maggots ooze from my vaginal lips, accompanied by a ridiculous amount of cum. The carpeting underneath me is becoming waterlogged in my jism. I feel my babies frolic and explore deep inside my cavity, causing mini spasms of pleasure as I lay back from the exertion, my body covered in sweat. A rasping moan escapes me as I am seized by another set of spectacular orgasms.

"*Fuuuuccckkkkk yyyyeeessss*!!!!" I squeal like a banshee. I came so hard that I bit my lip until it bled like a sieve down my cheek, like I was a savage quadruped.

A strong calm finally takes hold of me like a lover in a passionate embrace, and I feel infinitely better after pleasuring myself off that ledge of insanity I was hovering over. It Momentarily quelled this almost frantic anxiety gnawing at my frazzled psyche. This was just what the doctor ordered, if the doctor in question was a maniacal quack, of course! After I clean myself, I ponder what the morning will bring once Lux discovers the aftermath of our brutal battle with Pat Bale.

There will be consequences. I am just unsure if it is the slapped wrist kind, or the bullet in the head at point-blank range, buried out in a shallow grave in the middle of the desert kind. I decide to take a power nap to fully charge my depleted batteries, then I will go talk to

Lurch afterwards so that we can form a united front and build a believable story and game plan. It is a genuine possibility that we will soon have to fight for our very lives here.

Chapter Two

Desperately Seeking Morticia

I HAVE BEEN SEARCHING for her right about two long years with no luck until today. I was foraging some food from a landfill; it had been days since I fed on anything of sustenance when it happened. It was like a psychic distress beacon being blasted into my brain like a bullet from a highly powerful rifle from out of nowhere. I reeled from the pain, and viciously shook my head as if that would somehow dispel this interloper thought scrambling my psyche into Swiss cheese. Two words brilliantly flashed in my mind as if wrapped in Christmas lights, flashing, and strung out to an absurd length in my pummeled and perplexed mind.

"Fuuuuccckkkk yyyyeeessss!!!!" it incessantly intoned.

As if that was not enough proof, a spicy, fetid, and meaty aroma assaulted my sense of smell, one intermingled with lust and rot melded together in total unison. It was her. There could be no doubt of that now. I KNEW that stench better than anything! It was my very first memory of HER.

It fills me with a renewed sense of vigor and dedication for my purpose once again. She is my drive, and now I have the tools to seek her out once and for all...

Chapter Three

Kim Cleans Up

As I am being led into Lux's office by his flustered, nervous secretary, it's abundantly clear that shit has hit the proverbial fan here at H2TC headquarters. Just one glance at the CAM footage is all I need to see to know that a bloodbath had just ensued. If that was not enough of an indicator, then Lux's profuse sweating and his manic pacing is. After a full minute of me being there, he finally looks up and notices me. He grimaces at me while whipping his sweaty brow with what looks like a Gucci Bee pattern silk pocket square. Only $200, *what a steal*, I think to myself.

"Ah, Kim, thank God you are here now. I am at my wit's end with this whole situation." He says in his prissy and condescending tone.

"Yes, I can see that, Lux. It looks like WW3! What exactly went down here last night?"

"Um, yes, it is the unfortunate business of working with psychopaths. Regrettably for Mr. Bale, he could not leave well enough alone and faced the dire consequences of his choices."

As if on cue, he queued the video surveillance footage to Morticia, extracting this Pat Bale character's still-beating heart from his hemorrhaging and gaping anus. I hate that bitch with a passion, but I must give the devil her due on that one. The bitch is hard to the fucking core. Hard-Gore whore is a more apt title. I stare at the miniscule, expectant man staring at me, and secretly wish I could rend his face to ribbons with my bare hands, and stretch the tattered meat from his screaming face like gooey cheese from an exceptionally made pizza pie. But this sounds like he might have a job for me here. Best not to mutilate my new boss just yet, I guess reluctantly.

"I assume you want me to do damage control. Am I correct in that assumption, Lux?" He stared at me balefully before he replied.

"I hope you can help get things back to normal, or whatever normal passes for around this dungeon. Our buyers are, how shall I put it, highly impatient for new material to begin production again. With Pat, uh, gone, I am going to need Lurch to perform some of the more distasteful work. The *cheese pizza work*, if you get my meaning. I already have a strong feeling that he will refuse to do it, though. He is very particular about the work he will do."

"The child pornography? Yes, I get your innuendo, Lux. How do you want things handled if he refuses?" I ask, knowing the answer already.

"Then you will have to eliminate him, plain and simple. And if you must kill him, then I will have no choice but to have you kill Morticia as well. They have developed a strong bond working together and have become good friends."

"Two lunatic peas in a pod, huh?"

"To put it mildly, yes, Miss White. Now, once you end both parties, it leaves H2TC in a severe bind of sorts. I already have scouts out there looking for fresh talent, but one thing that has always been near impossible to find is quality female killers. Morticia Maggot blasted onto the scene with a vengeance and has been a big fan favorite here ever since her inception into our organization. Her sexy, gothic looks certainly do not hurt things with our clients, but it is her diabolical bloodlust that garnered the adoration of ALL our buyers. She is now worth a great sum of money to our syndicate. I have seen your handiwork for butchery, and I know they would absolutely love you. What would it take to get you on board here with us, Miss White?"

Wow, this was unexpected. Here I thought I was only doing a hit on some giant backwoods freak and that gothic cunt from hell. Being the new star of Hurt 2 The Core had a nice ring to it. I mentally pumped the brakes in my mind first. No sense in getting ahead of myself. I have my work cut out for me here. I am not delusional in that fact.

"You can call me Kim. I am not opposed to hearing your pitch, Lux, but let's see how this pans out first, though."

"Are you worried about getting killed?"

"Shit, if either of these pathetic cretins kills me in a dream, they better wake up and apologize. I do not get killed; I do the killing Lux."

"That is the answer I wanted to hear! I would like you to meet my head of security, feel free to use him to your discretion."

He paged the intercom and a moment later the spiritual successor to every action hero of the eighties strode in. He reminded me mostly of Arnold Schwarzenegger's character, John Matrix from Commando. Though he was vastly smaller than this Lurch creature, as almost anyone would be. But for a human, he was easily the biggest I have ever seen in real life. He carried an array of guns on his person and had an assault rifle strapped to him for good measure. He even had one of those Rambo knives on his hip! Overkill, to be sure, but we might need it tonight.

"Kim, this is my head of security, Chad Ripley. Chad, this is Kim White, our cleaner."

"Pleased to meet you, Kim. I look forward to working with you, and kicking some serious ass if need be!" he put his hand out to shake hands with me like we are long lost pals. Corded veins bulge in his forearms like burrowing night crawlers.

"Oh, I am sure it will be necessary to decimate these freaks, Chad. In fact, I can almost guarantee it."

A sly smile etched across his face at the mere mention of an altercation. I could tell already that conflict gets his dick harder than arithmetic. That's okay, it gets me wet as well. I want nothing impeding this inevitable showdown for me. Revenge for my brother is all that is driving me right now.

As we gripped one another's hands, he greeted mine firmly, but did not mangle my hand, which is rare when you must work in a masculine dominated field that enjoys swinging their little dick's around, constantly trying to be the alpha male in every scenario.

He had an air about him. I could tell right away he thought he was God's gift to women. He had a flirtatious smirk as he talked to me. Maybe if he played his cards right, I might give him a piece if I make it out of this alive. It is not like I doubt myself or my skills as a badass killing machine, but to think you are invincible is nothing but a losing game, to be sure. Besides, some good dick after turning Morticia into literal maggot food sounds like the best capper on this day, if you ask me!

"So, I assume you'll have this Lurch's answer by the afternoon, then?" I ask.

"Yes, indeed. We will do a conference call with him as soon as our meeting is over. I expect we will need your services immediately afterwards, so I would suggest remaining around the compound, please. We can order you some lunch. How does Dorsia sound?"

Just at the mere utterance of food, my stomach warbles in enthralled anticipation. Nothing like a full stomach before butchering human carcasses to a mangled pulp!

"I could eat. I heard the squid ravioli, in a lemon grass broth with goat cheese profiteroles, are to die for there!"

With a curt nod, Lux beckoned to his harried secretary to hurry and get the lunch order put in. I glanced back over to Chad, who was staring at himself in the full-length mirror. He was posing like he was taking part in a bodybuilder's competition. I chuckled inwardly as I watched him become lost within himself. He would probably suck his own dick if he could, I surmised. But to be fair, I am sure most men would if they could. Men are no better than dirty mongrels, after all.

My gaze went back to the security footage of Morticia and Lurch. The giant man caused me some alarm if I am being totally honest with myself. It is not every day that you see a human specimen that could portray a real-life superhero. The closet I have ever seen was Hafthor Bjornsson, easily one of the strongest men on the planet, so much so that he played The Mountain in Game of Thrones. This Lurch, though, He was easily two times bigger than Thor was. I was going to have my hands full with that monstrosity. My hate-filled gaze then panned to Morticia Maggot. I have spent so much time daydreaming her demise, and now it was almost within my oh so eager reach!

Seeing her giggling like a schoolgirl, and lightly slapping that walking freak show's impossibly immense biceps, while my poor brother festered away in some nameless pit, like a castaway piece of trash of no important significance. I was still seeing red for that goth trash b-list bimbo. Enjoy your time, what little you have left, with your overgrown Frankenstein's Monster. There is a new slaughter sheriff in town now, Morticia, and I am going to take extreme pride and care when it comes time to turning you into a human mulch pile of gore bitch.

Chapter Four

Choices, Or Lack Therof

Lurch and I have been up for around an hour, and were trying to come up with some sort of concrete game plan for last night's debacle, when Lux's voice boomed down at us like a vengeful, angry God from the intercom system.

"Morticia Maggot and Lurch Beauregard, report to the conference room for a video chat immediately!!"

"Welp, it sounds like our ass is grass. He used our first and last names. Daddy is pissed off at us, Lurch, baby," I faux pout with a smirk.

"I don'ts like the sound of this Miss Morticia, I smells a heap o'trouble for us," an exasperated Lurch laments.

"Let us get this show on the road, big boy. I believe we are about to get the most monumental ass chewing of our lives. But I have been chewed out by the best of 'em. I do not think that this mini-me mother fucker will measure up!"

Lurch momentarily laughs, no doubt from my visual, before reverting to his morose mug.

"I guess so. I've got this feelin' in my gut that keeps pesterin' me, and it ain't a good one!"

"Remember, Lurch, baby, that we got solidarity. If we must clean house with these fucks, then so be it. I would prefer we leave things amicably, but if they push us, best believe we are gonna push back, but harder and meaner!"

"Ya think we gots ta kill 'em?"

"Maybe, baby, that ain't such a bad thing, though, is it?"

"Ifs we's gotta, we's gotta, I suppose. I ain't lettin' 'em hurt you. You's my gal!"

This boy still can make me smile, even after all of this time.

"Lurch, baby, let me do all the talking, okay? You will only get flummoxed, and I do not want that." The big man only nodded in affirmation, his head hanging low like a regretful child's before a spanking.

Lurch seemed deep in contemplation, as if visualizing us massacring them in that oversized head of his. He nodded silently to himself, as if coming to a tough but necessary decision. He seemed fidgety, so I silently entwined his hand into mine as we walked into the conference room.

The minute Lurch and I wandered into the room, Lux was glaring incessantly at us via the vast television screen. He resembled a colossal leviathan looming over a cowering city, ready to stomp it all into oblivion. He had nothing but fuming contempt exuding from his smoldering gaze.

"Hey Luxie, what's up?" I coyly ask.

"Cut the cute girl act. You know goddamn well what is up. You and that dim bulb beside you massacred our biggest money maker. I have got a back load of 5 cheese pizzas that need filming ASAP, and no one to do it now!"

"Woah, Luxie, you even going to let me explain my side of what happened?"

"I know what happened. Bale went full psycho and was going to kill you both in a psychopathic frenzy. I watched the surveillance footage, remember?"

"Well then, you should know that our hands were tied. You couldn't have expected us to just take it up the ass and let him massacre us without a fight, right?"

"Morticia, I am not a moron, of course I know you did what you had to. It still does not release you from total fault, though. So, here is my proposal on what we do for the time being. Both of you listen up, snap that hillbilly retard out of whatever daydream he is under because this mostly pertains to him!"

That he called Lurch a retard really got my blood boiling, but I mentally counted to ten, so I do not pop off at the mouth like I am known for. I got a hotter head than that Mexican cartel gore video called Ghost Rider. Maybe what Lux is about to propose to us will not be so bad after all, right? I am Jack's cold sweat.

"So, here is what is going to happen. Morticia, for the time being, you will do all your normal videos plus Lurch's. I know you don't like killing women, but I, unfortunately, do not care at this juncture. As for The Incredible, dim-witted Hulk over there, he is doing all of Bale's tapes till we get an adequate replacement, capisce? Can you parlay that back to him so he will understand, dear?"

I immediately felt Lurch tense up and tremble uncontrollably from Lux's commands. He looked like Michael J. Fox on a really bad day! I tried to soothe him quietly, but I could tell he was going to say something almost immediately.

"Likes Hell, I am Mr. Lux. I ain't gonna hurt no babies or kids, no siree Bob! I's kill myself before I's ever lays a hand on an innocent child, you son-of-a-bitch!"

I continue trying to shush Lurch up as calmly as I can, to no avail. I look at Lux and shrug knowingly. A blind person could have seen this shit coming.

"Look, Lux, Lurch is not cut out for that type of killing and torturing. I know this for a fact. If you cannot find someone fast enough, well then, I guess I will have to do it."

With a petulant look on his cultured face, Lux simply said one word.

"No."

"Why the fuck not?" I say exasperatedly.

"Because this is how it is going to be, is why. It is his penance. This is an order and a punishment for the mess you both have made, and for all the financial trouble this has put me through. You will do as I say or face the very dire and deadly consequences. Do you both understand me?"

I got ready to spout some BS just to bide us a little more time when Lurch simply put an end to that idea with a quickness.

"I won't do it, and nothin's gunna make me do's it."

I looked worriedly from Lurch then back to Lux, sweat began pooling on my brow from the rollercoaster of emotions this meeting was doing to my psyche.

"Very well then." Lux said darkly, then the monitor went to black.

"I'm terribly sorry Miss Morticia, but I's could never do that."

"It is okay, bubba, but you know what this means now, right?"

"No ma'am."

My brain buzzed with an intense frenzy, like it was being swarmed with angry hornets. I looked to Lurch with an unholy ferocity smoldering in my eyes and growled in a guttural tone that I barely recognized.

"It's time to go to fucking war with these cunts!"

Chapter Five

Premonitions Of War

Lux's face looked as red as a slapped baby's ass when he angrily shut down the communication. Chad stood beside his boss, but I could not get a feel for his assessment of the situation. He was wearing a pair of aviator glasses like he was Maverick from Top Gun, for God's sakes. Lux started chortling to himself as if hearing a good joke in his mind and smiled at us, wide and eccentrically.

"It went exactly as I expected it would people. Kim, I need you to go down there and eradicate my problem for me. Take Chad with you and kill them both. Until I can arrange new talent, you will handle all the videos. Will that be an issue for you?"

"I was born to kill; my insatiable bloodlust knows no bounds, women and children, be damned, in my mind."

"Mozart to my ears, Kim. Okay, splendid, let us get this unfortunate business out of the way immediately, shall we? Chad, make sure and protect our new star. That is tremendously paramount. Is that understood?"

"Sir, yes sir, cannot wait to let off some steam like Bennett down there and fuck these two ingrates up properly."

As he rotated his neck, it painfully cracked like a snapped tree branch. I inwardly cringed. Did he just do a fucking *Commando* movie quote?

"Just as long as you know to follow my lead down there, I'm running this monkey show now. Will that be an issue for you, Chad?"

"No Ma'am." Chad agrees chipperly with an all too telling smirk of what he thinks about a strong woman bossing him around. Tough titty said the kitty, deal with it asshole, the future is very fucking female.

"Chad, you heard Kim. She is in charge. Make sure she makes it back in one piece and there will be an obscenely hefty bonus waiting for you in your bank account."

"No problem Lux, I got her back like I am a mother-fucking coat."

As we both head to the elevator, I wanted to run to it and quickly descend into the depths of this depraved domicile. My thirst for Morticia's blood was at a fever pitch now, an all-encompassing urge. Our uncertain destiny was but a mere moment away now.

I looked at Chad and expectantly. "Are you ready?" I asked point blank.

"Hell yeah! We are on an express elevator to Hell, going down!"

An *Aliens* quote now, really?

"That we are, Chad. Be on your toes. If we are indeed heading into Hell, then know this. That cunt Morticia Maggot would be Satan's right-hand woman! These two human-shaped fiends down there are natural born killers and are highly dangerous. Let us try to survive the night, shall we?"

Chad nods in silent agreement. He looks cool as a cucumber, which elevates my cockiness to an obscenely higher level than it already is.

I pressed the down button and head towards a fight I never would have dreamed of finally coming into fruition. The last I had seen of Morticia, we were in high school and I had left her crying in a fetal position, covered in maggots bawling her wimpy eyes out in the main hallway of our school. She was so weak back then. But now? The last thing I think of when it comes to her now is weakling. Ferocious is a more apt title. Grinning like a loon and drunk off the impending danger, I look at Chad maniacally.

"Abandon All Hope Ye Who Enter Here!"

Chapter Six

Making My Way Back To You

As I traversed my way towards her, a kind of "mind meld" again assaulted me. I saw a faint vision of her and a giant, scary man preparing for some sort of violent altercation, causing me to momentarily become light-headed and crash heavily into a desolate stretch of highway.

   A faint odor of adrenaline wafted towards my acute sense of smell. Our distance had been cut in half, if I had to venture a guess. I was pleased with my accomplishment, but now I was terrified for her well-being. I had to go faster so I could save her. With a renewed sense of purpose, I took off like a bat out of hell towards her. An incumbering wave of trepidation already crushing me under its immense weight as I speed towards my destination.

Chapter Seven

Bringing A Knife To A Gunfight

I STARE AT THE elevator, gripped in eagerness, as it descends to our vector. My fists ball so tightly my knuckles are bone white from the massive exertion. Lurch's chest heaves from the body dump of excessive amounts of epinephrine into his system. We are as ready as we ever can be, given the cards we have been dealt. I wield a gleaming, a razor-sharp machete as I take refuge behind a pillar. Lurch, sledgehammer employed in massive hand, made a quick B line to the adjacent pillar to prepare for whoever Lux was sending our way to kill us. I could give a fuck less who it is.

If Satan himself walked out, then his devilish ass was going to get carved the fuck up by my machete wielding ass. That or get his cranium crushed into a crimson, gore caked pulpy mess, by my big boy. The amber light on the elevator digits makes its silent countdown as we watch, as if we were fascinated by the glowing illumination. Lurch stares at me expectantly as our eyes meet. I make a kissy face at him and shout in excitement due to the impending battle at hand.

"Get ready baby, we both have to bring our 'A' game for whatever this is, or we are both as good as dead, and I do not plan on taking a dirt nap just yet!"

"Imma do everythin' I can to protect ya, Miss Morticia, even if it costs me my dadgum life!"

"I will not let it get to that point, bubba, I would kill everyone on the planet if that's what it took to save your life. Me and you are like peas and carrots, right? Just like Forest and Jenny!"

Bringing up his favorite movie was an act of pure brilliance on my part. Grit and determination immediately replaced any previous panic. We may have more sand than we do sense, but I'll be damned if we do not at least go down in a blaze of glory like that shitty Bon Jovi song.

"I love yuh, Miss Morticia."

"I love you too, Lurch, you ready?"

"Bout as much as a feller can be, I reckon."

"Same here, minus the feller part!"

We both get to giggling like a couple of goofballs from my wisecrack, probably a last-ditch effort to expel some extra nervous energy before the fight of our lives takes place. I look to the elevator and see it is on the first floor now, just one more floor before shit literally is going to hit the proverbial fan for us. In what feels like an absolute eternity, the elevator finally reached its destination. I take a deep breath and hold it in my lungs before expelling it out like a powerful hit of weed, along with the last vestiges of fear lingering in my reeling mind.

"Let's do the damned thing," I bellow like a crazed battalion sergeant trying to rouse their infantry to battle.

The elevator dings as if in retort to my battle-cry, and the doors open wide like a whore's legs in anticipation of receiving a rigid cock. At first, I credulously thought the elevator was empty, like maybe we just experienced a faux pas or some shit like that. Then I see a muscled forearm lob a pair of flash bangs into the center of the room with a loud clatter. Before Lurch and I can do anything, a blinding flash of light activated my photoreceptor cells in my eyes, blinding me for five seconds. I tried to shake off the effects of the device, but an afterimage is still impairing my vision. *I am Jack's worthless sight!*

My hearing was not fairing any better; the detonation has, of course, given me temporary fucking deafness, and if that was not enough strife already, it disturbed the fluid in my ear, causing a loss of balance to boot. So now your girl is temporarily blind and clumsy to boot. A shitty situation to be in when you have got the fight of your life in front of you. Real life Rocky and Apollo uphill type of battle going on here now, dammit!

I take a gander the best I can over at poor Lurch, who was obviously suffering from the same malaise as I am. He was hunched over, trying to feel his way around when the gunman casually stepped out of the elevator. He lobbed a smoke grenade into the room this time, dwindling our chances of survival even more. I have seen this movie quoting, neanderthal before, Chad, I think the dick-weed's name is. He is always standing behind Lux during most video calls, looking like a total douche bag-bro-dude every damn time.

I get a glimpse of the weapon that Chad has brought to this battle, and like the old Mafia Don's used to say, he came fucking heavy. In his grubby mitts, the arrogant prick carries a Colt M4 Carbine assault rifle, which has the proud moniker of "One of the defining firearms of the 21st century."

With a rate of fire of 700+ rounds a minute, we have to take this alpha asshole down fast with only cutting weapons and brute force. Yeah, this is going to be a barrel of laughs and a cakewalk. Easy peasy, lemon squeezy!

I quickly crab walk over to Lurch and direct him further down into the cafeteria area before dickface can mow us down in a hail of gunfire like some Columbine Trench coat Mafia loser. I need to shout at him because of the aftereffects of the flash grenade. We can have the illusion of cover if he helps me turn the table to the side. Almost immediately after, the bastard open fires on us. The heavy artillery sound of a powerful machine gun creates a deafening wall of sound, as does the plummeting sound of countless spent shell casings.

I look to Lurch and bawl, "We need to stop that asshat from being able to shoot for a minute so we can fuck his ass up! Do you think you can hit him with the machete? Don't you country bumpkins have a knack for knife throwing and shit like that?" I say with a playful grin.

"Yessum, I think I kin hit the sucker with that there machete. I's pretty sure I can take out his shootin' arm, too!"

"Lurch, you beautiful bastard, I could kiss you!"

I immediately do so, planting one on top of his bulbous head. The smell of gunpowder is overwhelming, as is the smoke from Chad's relentless gunfire assault. A haze begins to permeate our battle field with acrid smoke like the smog in Los Angeles. I hand him my blade and watch in amazement as Lurch closes his little grape sized eye, while that gargantuan, creepy orb of his stares directly at Chad, and waits for him to cease fire. After what feels like an eternity, he finally runs out of ammo. He fishes into his vest, frantically grabbing for another clip, when I yell hoarsely to Lurch.

Do it now, you big, beautiful bastard!"

With little to no hesitation, Lurch hurls the machete with the speed and accuracy of a stealth missile. The blade hurtles towards Chad like a javelin thrown by the fucking Terminator! I watch in awe as I see Chad do his best 80s action hero mimicry, yelling like Stallone in Rambo part three! He sprays round after round in our general direction, hoping to kill us with no real form of confrontation. He is obviously a chicken shit. Unfortunately for him, Lurch and I do not play that shit. We thrive on getting all up in a fucker's face and making their deaths ultra-personal and nasty.

Before Chad's stupid ass even realizes what is happening, the machete plunges into his left shoulder, sinking deep into the meaty tissue with the ease of a hot knife sliding through warm butter. A look of utter shock is etched upon his idiotic face as he wails in agony from the devastating wound. With a slap on his back, I yell to Lurch to with malicious glee.

"Attack that bitch hog! Teach him what happens if someone fucks with us!"

With an unnerving, for his size, quickness, Lurch lunges forward, sledgehammer in tow as he makes his move. Before Chad can do anything besides recoil and bleed, Lurch materializes in front of him like the Grim Reaper himself. I see that the sight of my big boy in person is too much for this gun toting pussy to handle, and begin to hoot in delight as he pisses himself in fear of his impending death. Lurch stares at this new development with a look of disgust and says to the pallid, quavering man.

"Mr. Chad, that is just plain gross! What is ya, a big ole' baby or somethin'?"

And before Chad knows what hit him (get it?) the fifteen-pound sledge comes crashing down on top of his kneecap, obliterating the cartilage into fragments and scattering the meniscus into the far corner of the room. Lurch raises the mallet once again like he was John Henry working on the railroad, and batters his other kneecap into a mushy pulp to match the other. He falls heavily to the ground and writhes around in exquisite agony. His decimated knees are horribly mangled, spewing blood onto the floor in rapid spurts.

Once again, the hammer is raised, and again it crashes into Chad's body. This time the blow plows into his abdomen, immediately making him throw up a geyser of blood, so dark it looks black. He also retches out what looks like a bunch of giant clots as well as whatever he last ate into a steamy pile of slop on his chest and shoulder. With one last mighty swing, Lurch sends the weighted head crashing directly on top of Chad's head with a thunderous *CCC-RRR-AAA-CCC*-KKK sound!

The force of the strike shatters Chad's skull like a fine China plate, and imbeds the weighted mallet deep within his cranium, bursting through all three layers of his meninges membranes. His brain matter spews out of his ears and even pours out of his eyes after the devastating kill shot erupts his eyeballs right out of their sockets from the savage force of the strike. Chad's neck takes on the characteristics of a tortoise, descending deeply into his body as the brutal hammer blow forces his head and neck down into his chest cavity, dislodging his heart. His body takes on a herky-jerky type of epileptic fit, as his frame spasms out of control.

Blood fountains out of his face like a faucet left on full blast as he continues to screech like a cat being set on fire by a psychopathic youth. Lurch chuckles to himself before bringing the hammer down a final time, splattering Chad's head into more pieces than I thought was humanly possible, like a dropped porcelain statue from a great height. A final death rattle escapes his smashed head, a gurgling sound from the back of his throat, thus ending his worthless existence once and for all.

"Damn, Lurch, I didn't expect you to recreate a Cannibal Corpse track with Chad, but Hammer Smashed Face is definitely a classic track of brutality!"

"You's know I don't git any of yer pop culture references, Miss Mortica."

"I'm sorry, bubba, I forgot you only listen to Conway Twitty!"

"I's like me sum Hank Williams Sr, and Merle Haggard too!"

"My apologies for besmirching your musical tastes, bubba."

"I's gonna let it slide fer once." Lurch responds with a chortle.

"I'm just glad you are safe, buddy."

"Same here, Miss Mortica. I loves yuh and glad you ain't hurt neither!"

We look at each other and begin laughing like a couple of schoolgirls talking about a cute boy. Lurch is standing in front of the elevator when it happens in a flash. A lithe figure slithers from out of the elevator doors, masked by the massive amount of lingering gun smoke like a stealthy ninja before either of us knew what was happening. They scrambled up Lurch's back faster than a cockroach scurrying away from a light source. Once they were atop of Lurch's massive shoulders, I could finally get a guise of this dangerous new interloper. A look of recognition, interlaced with shock, blanketed my face like a cold winter's night as she sneered at me triumphantly.

"I guess you should have investigated the elevator before you guys started sucking your own dick's first, huh? I knew I should have killed you back in high school. But do not fret, it is not a mistake I am going to make twice. And if it is any sort of consolation to you, your fugly bestie here can join you!"

I watched in total agony as Kim-Fucking-White, bitch supreme, raises her weapon high above her as she evades Lurch's grasping digits.

"This is for killing my brother, you basic-bitch-goth-cunt!"

Kim stabs Lurch repeatedly in his neck with an ice pick as I stand frozen rigidly in place, like a statue. Lurch's face contorts in pure agony as he looks at me in a panic. He wordlessly pleads for me to do something, anything, but I cannot. It is almost like the resurgence of this brutal bully has triggered my PTSD, shutting me completely down. Kim excitedly stabs his throat repetitively with a blinding speed that seems almost unreal. *CGI, it must be special effects.*

"H-e-e-e-elllllppppppp, Miss Morticia, get this dadgummed varmint offa meeeeee!!!"

Lurch desperately tries to pry Kim off him, but the immense blood raining down has caused her to be way too slippery for him to grasp for more than a second at a time. He finally grabs a hold of her and looks triumphant, if only for a moment. Kim scoffs at this and stabs my poor boy's hand repeatedly until he relinquishes his hold on her.

I feel like I am rooted in place, like an ancient and gnarled tree, watching my best friend being slaughtered right in front of me. Seeing that snarky, uppity cunt's face after all these years is like a blast to the face from a bucket of frigid ice water. It sends me careening back into time, to the last day I saw Kim in high school and the prank she pulled on me before I left high school forever. Back to the day I discovered my disgusting filth-fetish for inserting creepy crawlies into my joy trail for pleasure for the first time.

    I am thinking about all these things in nanoseconds. I need to snap out of this fugue state and save my friend, but my brain is willing me back in time to relive this incessant flashback. I surrender to its demand and let go. It is time to revisit my past so I can get back to the present before it is too late for Lurch...

Chapter Eight

Roll That Flashback Footage

As I enter the Halls of Theodore Robert Bundy High School, I am immediately assaulted by the looks of disparagement from the preppy and the jock kids. I mean, I can't really blame them, I guess; I look like I went to Hot Topic and bought the goth girl starter kit, for fuck's sake. My hair is jet black, as is my lipstick and fingernails. All to match my heart, of course. I am rocking a Marilyn Manson Antichrist Superstar shirt, a black miniskirt, and a ridiculous pair of Doc Martens that resemble a pair of boots that Herman Munster might wear.

I ignore their provocative sneers and filthy catcalls and slink off to my locker like a petrified rabbit trying to get to its hole. After entering my combination into my locker, I look at all the artwork and pictures that adorn my little slice of Heaven in this hellish cesspool, and silently count to ten so I can dispel some of this crippling anxiety being here bombarded me with. Plus, it gives me a little extra time for flirting with my despair, before heading to first period and dealing with all these shitty sycophants for the entire day.

As I am preparing to turn around, I feel a presence skulking behind me. I do not need to be a fortune teller to fathom a guess on who it is. It is the bitchy bane of my existence at Ted Bundy High School. It is Kim White and her group of lackey cunts from hell. I already feel my blood boil. I am Jack's medulla oblongata.

"Well, if it isn't the scuzziest cooze in the entire school. How's the queen of the trailer park doing so far today?" Kim yipped in her typical cunty demeanor.

Her mindless squad of cretin's snigger at her "joke" like she is the funniest person alive. The shittiest person alive is a more apt title, if you ask me.

"I was doing good until you arrived," I said. "Don't you guys have a bukkake blowbang or something to get to? I am kind of busy here, if you do not mind. "

"Busy being a fucking loser!" A nameless lemming quips.

I suppose they were hoping to get an attagirl from her. Kim barely batted an eye before she went in on me again, to the delight of the crowd forming around us. When you are the queen bee of the school, like Kim is at this retched shit-hole, you garner an audience everywhere you go.

"C'mon guys, cut Morticia some slack, she has probably been up all-night, giving dude's hand jobs underneath the overpass so she can afford to eat, being that she does not have a daddy and her momma is a candidate for the next season of 600 Pound Life. As a matter of fact, we have a present for you!"

I do not even try to stick around for any more of their ugly rhetoric towards me. It was not even original material, just the same recycled, regurgitated garbage shit-talk they spew from their hateful mouths every other day or so to me. I slammed my locker shut and did not even bother zipping up my backpack as I trekked past the gawkers with their phones out, recording my misery porn like it was the highest form of entertainment imaginable.

"That's alright, Kim, you can keep whatever gift you were going to give me. I don't need your charity, nor do I even want it!" I huffed in exasperation.

"Oh, but I insist! I believe in being charitable to the downtrodden denizens of our town, much like yourself!" Kim purred in mock hurt.

"Sell that shit to someone buying it, because I sure the fuck am not!" I retort icily.

I tried to walk faster. I just needed to get to Algebra one, and that was only a few more yards away. I would at least get an hour breather from these malcontent bitches. The doorknob was mere inches from my reach when it happened. These twats dumped a five-gallon bucket on top of my head, sending its foul contents raining down upon me like rain in a deluge. Maggots, it was a bucket full of writhing, pale maggots. Of course, it had to be fucking maggots. I am Jack's complete lack of surprise.

It felt like everything went silent for a moment in the hallway, like when you press mute on your remote control during a loud infomercial. Then it was like a levee broke wide open, flooding a torrent of cruel guffaws upon me, drowning me in their collective cruelty. I gaze helplessly at their harsh, leering faces as they point at me like I was a sideshow. I miserably sought some way of refuge to escape their taunts and jeers as the squirming vermin I was coated in plummeted from my quaking form to the ground with an audible plopping sound. I shook myself furiously like a wet dog, sending the grubs in every direction possible. I was drenched in them, though. I could feel them writhing in my hair, hopelessly imbedded in every nook and cranny of my body. I must get out of here and shower, to cleanse myself of this putridity.

"Make sure to pick up every maggot now, Morticia. I would hate for you to go without a meal. These things have plenty of protein, I have heard. Maybe it will help make your tits grow some? God knows you need it, since you are flatter than a board!" Kim cackled with nefarious delight.

I felt like Carrie at the prom, being ridiculed by these clueless fucks. Dammit, why can't I have telekinesis so I can slaughter everyone and reduce them to nothing more than gooey paste on the hallway floor? It doesn't really matter though; these pricks cannot kill me in a way that truly matters. These cretins are sub-basement basic bitches and I am an elevated bitch. I grab my grub-filled backpack and traverse towards the front door, middle fingers raised the whole time. I do not belong here; I feel just like that overplayed Radiohead song that never truly leaves anyone's minds. As the doors to my high school close behind me, it thankfully quells the deafening cat-calls that try to follow me out like a sketchy stalker.

Once I arrive at my ramshackle shit-box that I like to affectionately call home, I immediately strip off all my soiled clothes and stare at my nude form in my mirror in dismay. Kim's right. I hate my non-existent breasts. It dismays me that psycho barbie knew that was an Achilles' heel for me. It is like that no-good cunt had a window into my soul or some shit. I turn so I can look at my rump and give it a curt nod. At least I have a whooty, for fuck's sake! I allow myself an ever so brief twerk and laugh to myself at the utter absurdity of this entire scene.

My laughter is quickly replaced with an almost animalistic impulse to fondle and debase myself with a frenzied urgency that came out of nowhere. It felt like a direct response to the taunting I just endured from Kim and her motley crew of clueless cunts. They want me to feel like an ugly duckling simply because I do not fit into their views of attractiveness. I do not resemble a spray-tanned, collagen lipped, infused, bleach blonde harlot, so of course, I can't be pretty in their skewed perspective.

I aggressively squeeze my tits as I simultaneously tweak my aching nipples between my pointer fingers and thumbs. As I work myself into a sexual frenzy, I felt my cunny relinquish a bit of cum down my inner thighs. My digits probe my sex in earnest as I rake at my vagina with the tenacity of a cat on a scratching post going to town. I yank strands of my pubic hair out with my bare hands as I continue to frig myself uncontrollably. This feels exquisite and all, but it is not enough.

I want to fill my drooling axe-wound up to the brim, till it is bursting like a flimsy trash bag from the Dollar Tree, but what do I debase myself with? I have some decent dildos in a shoe-box I keep hidden under my bed that I stole from my momma back when sex was important to her. Now she would rather stuff her mouth with Twinkie's than fake dicks in her fat muff. The faux dick just is not blasphemous enough for my palate today, so that won't cut it. No siree Bob! A broom handle? Nah. An overly ripe squishy cucumber? Ewww, as if! Those bitches at school think I am a gross and deranged goth trailer trash? I will give them gross and deranged trailer trash all right, and then some! After all, I am from Missouri and we are not called the *Show Me State* for nothing, bubba!

Without thinking or even the slightest hesitation, I reach into my backpack and grab a massive handful of the slimy, putrid maggots in my eager hands and without contemplating why, I cram my entire hand into my frothing, rabid pussy and deposit a mega-ton of maggots into my aching cavern.

"Holy fucking-shit-this-feels-so-fucking-goooood!" I bellow out in a lust-infused screech of pleasure intermingled with shame. I sound like someone mimicking an XXX exorcism parody for fuck's sake, but I don't care. To quote my idol, Patrick Bateman, "*I feel lethal, on the verge of frenzy.*"

My pulsating box churns forth copious amounts of my jism intermingled with vermin as the coagulated concoction begins to faucet out of my cunt in earnest. With wild abandon, I grab even more maggots by the handful, shoveling them into my cunt like a backhoe excavating dirt at a job site at a frenetic, blistering pace.

"Come to mother, my beautiful babies, get into your new, warm, wet home." I snarl seductively.

Load upon load of the wriggling bastards get stuffed deep inside of my gaping twat as I make more of those weird bestial noises that remind me of a dog being run over repeatedly by an immoral child on a big wheel. I feel the familiar feeling of me about to cum yet again, but this time it is on a whole other level, and it is going to be a gusher. My body tenses as I reach the threshold of pleasure and begin screaming like a banshee. I am Jack's monumental orgasm!

After I regain my senses from all the copious cumming, I get up to head to the bathroom. Bodily fluids and critters galore plop to the ground as I prepare to shower off all this ick coated on my glistening form. I suddenly feel immensely creepy about what I have just subjected myself to. I take a scalding-hot shower that reddens my flesh like a massive sunburn, and even though I am sparkling clean on the outside, no amount of scrubbing will cleanse off this miasma of mortification tethered to my soul.

Once I am dressed, I get on the web and try to discover what I just did to myself, and if it even has a name. Insanity perhaps? After some intense Encyclopedia Brown cosplaying and interwebz surfing, I discover it. Apparently I have a fetish called Polyembolokoilamania. Sheesh, say that fucker three times as fast as you can! Its definition is *the act of inserting foreign bodies into orifices such as the rectum or vagina. Patients with Smith-Magenis syndrome exhibit it when motivated by a desire for sexual gratification.* TL; DR= I AM A SICK, DEGENERATE CUNT!!!

I get into my bed to go to sleep, but slumber evades me like an experienced boxer dodging jabs. I just kept picturing Kim deriding me, and how for as long as I have known her, even all the way back in elementary school, she had made it her life mission to hurt me as frequently as humanly possible. I cry and shake uncontrollably, reminiscing about all the hurt she had heaped upon me all these years. It was like she was constantly trying to kill me and a handful of other social outcasts that she targeted at our school. And in a sense, we all got killed, in every important way except the physical one.

I knew right there that I was never going back to school ever again. I knew something else, too. If I ever saw Kim White again, either I was going to kill her or she was going to kill me. I would never be someone's doormat again.

Chapter Nine

Losing Lurch

Me and Miss Morticia were in the middle of a big ole gigglin' spell about killin' that igit Mr. Chad, when this purty gal shot outta the gun smoke filled elevator and climbed atop me faster than a dad-gummed spider-monkey and began stabbing' me! Lordy, it hurts! I went to grab her cracker ass off me, but she skittered faster than a cockroach with the lights on and zigged when I's jagged and kept on stabbing'.

"Dadgummit, c'mere, so I can pulverize ya!"

"Shut up mutant freak, you want me? You are going to have to catch me, asshole!"

"Miss Morticia, help me grab this damn varmint!"

"No one can save you now. Your ass is mine, you ugly wretch. Your stupid bitch of a friend is next!"

I tried to holler' to Miss Morticia, but she looked like a zombie or somethin'. I could see tears rolling' down her cheeks, but it was like she was far aways or somethin'. I don't have the words to explain it no's better.

It was like in the movies. Ya know how time is slow as tar? Like a nightmare, I s'pose. I could see Miss Morticia staring at me, one second ago we were laughin', now her face is pale and her lip is tremblin' as it look like she's saying' somethin' but alls I can hear is the whooshing of the air as whoever this varmint is keeps stabbing' me to death! I bellow in fear and pain to anyone, someone to help.

"Lordy, Miss Morticia, help me!!!"

It's like she is stuck in place. She looks petrified or somethin', like she's seen a ghost. Then from behinds me, my attacker laughs like a damn witch in my ear. She gives it a lick, which is confusing to me. Miss Morticia stares at whoever this is behind me with a look of anger, the likes of which Mr Bale never gots! Suddenly, it's like she snaps outta of it and says somethin'. It is hard for me to make out though. I am coated in my blood and feeling' bad all of a sudden. Everything around me is dim, like the lights are getting' turnt off.

"Look, Kim, this is between me and you. Leave Lurch out of this. You want to fight someone, fight me. He is hurt bad, but I can still save him." Miss Morticia pleads.

So, the person killing' me is Miss Kim White? Miss Morticia has mentioned her before in our talks. She was always pickin' on Miss Morticia when they were young. I hurtle myself towards the nearest wall, but I waited to dang long like the dummy I am. I couldn't hit it with enough strength to knock her off me or hurt her. I only fall to the ground after on accounts of me knockin' my noggin against the wall. She just scuttled to the other side of me to not get hurt!

"I am telling you now, Kim. Stop now and let me tend to his wounds or you are ten seconds away from feeling hell's wrath!" Miss Morticia screams!

"Bitch, this is on you, not me. You killed my brother who, although a piece of shit, I loved dearly. You kill someone I loved, now I kill someone you loved. Tit for tat, cunt."

I feel a powerful hurt as Miss Kim buries that icepick to the hilt into the side of my neck. I feel hot blood shooting outta me like pecker snot.

"NO! NO! NO! NO! NNNNN-OOOOO!" Miss Morticia hollers!

With my last bit of might, I finally catch her with my bare hands, and wrap her long, blonde hair in a death grip, and fling her into the far wall as hard as I can with a loud, meaty smack. She falls to the ground and doesn't move a stitch. I'm feelin' awfully woozy now. My legs can barely hold me up. I fall heavily to my knees as Miss Morticia rushes to me and gently lays me down. She looks at me, all worried-like.

"You're hurt bad, buddy, but I am with you now."

She's lookin' right into my eyes and her tears are steadily plopping' onto my face as she hugs and shushes me like I'm her baby or somethin'. I hug her back and kiss her flushed cheek. I's looks around the room and it reminds me like a damned tornader hit it. We are stuck down here. The only ways out was the elevator, but once the doors closed, it takes a visual OK from someone up yonder to let the elevator to come back down agains. I stare at the one window that's protected by steel bars and know what I gots to do now. I get up, makin' Miss Morticia try an' stop me, but I gently but firmly push her back.

"You have to rest, baby; you're hurt awfully bad."

"Miss Morticia, I gots an idea to get you outta here."

"Just rest, bubba, I will figure out a way later. I must keep your neck compressed; you are bleeding like a stuck pig."

"I don't matter no more. I's gotta get you outta here so you don't get killed by that wild woman."

As I get up, I can feel the blood from my neck wound flow like a faucet. I ain't gots much time. I hurry to the window and yank at the steel bars with all my might. I strain and holler as I work on it. At first, it feels like nuthin' happens. I can feel myself growing weaker and know it's now or never. I picture Poor Miss Morticia getting' kilt down here cuz I couldn't save her, somethin' I swore to do! I start crying, but I also get real mad too! I mustered up my gumption and began again, using my love for this gal as fuel to give it one last shot!

I could feel it give now! I pulled harder, like I got a power surge or something! You know what? Love is the most powerful emotion there is, I think. Some think it is hate, but they are plumb wrong! I feel dang near every vein cord and pulse with the little blood I gots left in me as I continue to pull as hard as I can. Inch by inch, the steel barrier comes loose! I could feel the skin tearing away from my fingertips and palms, but I kept on pulling. With one last yank and a grunt, I dig deep and use the last of my strength and the thought of Miss Morticia getting outta this dad gummed hell-hole. and the bars finally bust free, taking down a good portion of the wall, too. The surprise of it givin' way sends me fallin' to the floor hard on my rump. I can't even see properly no more, but I's did it. My girl can go now. I kept my promise to my angel.

"I did it, Miss Morticia. I didn't let you down fer once."

"You could never let me down, baby. I am so proud of you!"

She smiles at me, but she looks a mess. She is still crying real hard and snottin' like a baby, and it pains me to be the blame of her hurt.

"I loves ya, Miss Morticia, I need you to be free and git far away from this nightmare place."

"I can't just leave you here. Maybe there is time left to save you if we try to make it to a hospital or something?" She sniffles as she caresses my forehead.

"I's a goner, Miss Morticia. I don't think I can even move no more. But imma stay inside your heart forever and ever. Maybe you could get to my place in Cowgill and lives there. That would do my heart good, to know you have a safe space. That way, it would be like I did somethin' good for ya."

"Lurch baby, you have always done good stuff for me. You are my best friend. I do not think I have ever loved another human being in my whole life, or was even capable of it, until I met you. I am not ashamed to say that I love you with all my heart. After I kill Kim White and avenge your death, I'll go to Cowgill."

"Livin' is what I's wants yuh to do. That's my dream for you, Miss Morticia."

She openly sobs as she holds me against her and kisses my cheek.

"So that was Miss Kim, huh?"

"Y-Y-es, it was." She doesn't seem to be able to say much. She is trying to hide her cries from me, I s'pose.

"Shee-it, she is meaner than a basket of rattlesnakes!" I say with a smile and a laugh, even though it pains me to do so.

You can't always help how you go out in this crazy world, but I want to do it with bravery and try to not let Miss Morticia feel so scared about it. I grab her hand and squeeze it tightly with the last bit of strength I got. She looks at me with scared, teary eyes and I give her my best smile.

"I love you, git on outta here. Go and live yourself a long, happy life. I's alway will be watchin' over you... I loves ya friend."

And with that, I feel my eyes close and I fade away.

Then I feel all kinds of weird. It's like I can now see myself and Miss Morticia like I am lookin' down on us from above. It's like I am floatin' up and away like a balloon! When I take a gander up, it looks like I am headin' down a long white tunnel. I am bathed in this light and it feels nice and calmin' like. I guess I's heading to the pearly gates I's always heard about. I look down again and see Miss Morticia hold me tightly, kissing me all over my face, and bawling over me still, poor thing. I hate leaving her now when the journey isn't done yet for her. Hopefully, I kilt that mean Miss Kim that was stabbing me when I flung her against the wall. With a last look below, I blow Miss Morticia a kiss and turn toward the tunnel. Unsure where it will take me, I push forward into the light, toward my destiny.

Chapter Ten

Become Wrath

My big, beautiful boy is dead. The last bit of his life fluid drain out from his severed jugular vein from Kim's excessive stabs. His eyes stare at me, past me, looking at everything and seeing nothing all at once. A minute ago, we were laughing. Now he is nothing but an empty husk lying in front of me. Why is it that all everything I love gets violently taken from me? Why must I always be alone? I close his eyes with my fingertips, his one tiny grape eye, and his enormous, grapefruit sized orb. With a sudden rage, I pound the ground with my fists until it hurts. But I do not want to hurt myself. Oh no. I want to destroy something beautiful.

Kim is beautiful on the outside. On the inside, though, she resembles a rancid, rotting corpse. I rise to my feet and head to the area where my big, lunkheaded boy threw her like the piece of trash that she is. If she is indeed dead, then I will just have a good old time dismantling her corpse, but if she is still alive? Then boy oh boy, I am going to make her suffer until her very last breath.

I get to her prone form and kick her as hard as I can muster. She groans lightly and I grin ear to ear at the lovely sound of her pain and discomfort. That means that she is not dead. That means that I get to become vengeance. I can become wrath incarnate for Lurch. That means I finally can retaliate for all those years in school where she made me feel less than. This is for making me even fleetingly consider suicide at one point in my life. This is to crush any potential I might have had by making me turn into an introvert from your constant and baseless harassment.

I grab the stupid bitch by her throat and lift her up slightly so that her back is resting against the wall. I can tell she is playing possum, so I give her two hellacious slaps to her face in rapid succession. That does the trick, instantly causing her to open her eyes and grimace at me as I glare down at her in disdain. She looks at me coldly, and it sends chills down my spine.

"By that furious look in your eyes, I guess that fugly creature, boyfriend, whatever of yours, must have kicked the proverbial bucket? It does not surprise me; you never could get yourself or keep a man, you fucking freak. If I would not have killed him, he would have deserted your nutso ass, regardless!"

She looks hideous, smiling at me about Lurch's death with thin blood trails weeping down her lips. I ball my fist so tightly that the skin becomes bone-white. I let loose with a haymaker punch to the side of her temple that knocks that snooty look right off her fucking smug face and dazes her immediately. Her eyes swim for a moment before they come back into focus. She snarls at me like a cornered animal, baring her teeth like a feral thing at me menacingly.

"What's it going to be then, eh?" Kim rasps furiously at me.

I raise my hand to strike her again, and that is when I hear a gun report go off. Immediately, the slug penetrates my shoulder and sends me careening over an overturned table. Holding my wounded shoulder, I glance over the side of the table and see that Lux has come down and apparently cut his losses on the whole deal. Maybe he originally intended Kim to kill us both, but since it appears I had the no-good bitch in my cross-hairs, he must have decided to intervene.

I am bleeding like a sieve over here, and am in no shape to battle this prick. My only hope is to get out of the escape window Lurch created for me and hope that Lux shoots Kim. I know one thing though, if I do not get this wound attended to, I will join Lurch in the by and by soon enough!

I can see Lux making his way to where I was only moments ago. I still see Kim over there as well, so I quickly fling a piece of metal in their general direction, startling Lux and making him shoot in that general direction. *It's now or never,* I think, propelling myself toward the only available escape route as fast as I can manage. Before Lux even has a chance, I dive out of the window like I am fucking Greg Louganis in his prime. Shit, put my ass on a Wheaties box now! I land with a crash into a trash-strewn alleyway, hurting my knee. Slowly, I get up on my shaking legs. I feel like a sailor at sea in a raging storm, rocking back and forth like a drunkard.

As I head the only way I can, I leave a trail of blood behind me. I limp out into the main street and grope my way past the darkened homes in a panic. How am I in the most desolate area possible? There is absolutely no one around, no cars, no homeless people. I do not even see any stray dogs or cats, for fuck's sakes! I continue my trek in earnest. I am Jack's unyielding tenacity.

    I walk, or more aptly, shuffle my way down the desolate stretch of road. I am exhausted, but I see a literal light at the end of my tunnel. It is a streetlight at the next corner. And it looks like a young girl is vaping while looking at her phone. The light illuminates her young face as she stares at her phone intently. She does not see me until I am upon her. I reach out to the girl, startling her. I go to say something, but I am robbed of my voice, and can only emit a weak squeaking sound before I fall to the concrete. Rolling over on my back, I stare up at the night sky and cannot help but wonder if Lurch is up there somewhere. The terrified girl stares at me, worry plastered on her face.

    "Hey lady, are you like... alright?" she asks hesitantly.

    "I am a million miles from okay, girlie." I say with a raspy chuckle and then pass out.

Chapter Eleven

Kim Deals Damage

I CANNOT BELIEVE THAT bootleg Elvira got away thanks to Lux fucking up the plan. I mean, sure, I guess one could argue that I looked like I was in a teensy bit of trouble, but I have been in way worse and prevailed, bet your bottom dollar on that shit! I get on my hands and knees and quietly crawl over to where Chad's corpse is laying and wrench the machete out of his worthless carcass. Then I spit in his face for royally fucking up this job. All he had to do was to shoot proficiently, and he could not do even that right. Typical male fuck up. That is why you always send in a woman to do the job right the first time!

   I watch as Lux makes his way to my original spot and is shocked to not find me there anymore. He cautiously bends down and touches the blood smear with his fingers and then stares at them wonderingly. This is where I strike him. Running full force, I slam into his shocked form like a SWAT team battering ram, sending him violently crashing into the wall with bone-jarring force, causing the gun to go soaring off to a far corner of the facility. I spin the old fuck around to look me eye to eye. He has a large gash on his forehead that is carpeting blood down his pale face as he stares at me, wide-eyed with fear.

"I had Morticia in the palm of my hands, and you had to come in and fuck it all up. I killed Lurch, and I had lulled her into a false sense of security. A moment later and I would have had her. Well, someone is going to die right now. Want to guess who that is, Lux? I will give you three guesses and the first two don't count."

"N-n-n-o-w wait just a second, Kim, there is no need to kill me, I only wanted to make sure you got her is all. I was, like, your contingency plan. That's all!"

"Bullshit, you old codger. You were just going to rid yourself of all of us and start over. I should have seen that coming. Fool me once, shame on you. Fool me twice, shame on me. There will not be a third time, Lux."

"W-w-w-wait a minute, young lady, I will pay you whatever you want, you have my word, a King's ransom, I promise to you!"

"Your word means fuck all to me now, gramps. Now shut your trap and take your medicine!"

Before Lux can babble any more of his bullshit, I belt him good and hard in his mouth with a deft punch, breaking his feeble jaw. It grotesquely hangs like a broken cabinet door, while an inundation of blood and teeth plunge from his orifice, clattering to the hard floor. He shrieks like an incoherent imbecile and pisses his slacks from fear of his upcoming violent demise.

"I hope this hurts you." I say, with a voice saturated with venom. Taking out my icepick, I jam it deeply in his left knee, up to the handle. Then, I stomp on it until it fully descends deep inside his kneecap. Blood erupts like lava from a volcano from the ruined knee joint.

Lux howls in delicious agony, which I, of course, eat up with great relish. As I decide what to do with the old bastard, I grip the machete in my hands. I remember watching an ultra-brutal cartel execution video on the subreddit, r/watchpeopledie, where an unseen person hacks a hapless victim into pieces.

I stare down at the quivering old man like he is nothing to me, which he is if I am being honest. My cold eyes bore into his, causing Lux to look away like the fearful little rabbit he truly is. "I'm going to kill you now, Lux." I say without a hint of remorse. "And it is going to be a very slow and painful process."

I raise the weapon above my head, ready to strike at any moment like an agitated anaconda. Lux puts up his hands in a defensive gesture and pleads for his life, showing some real passion.

"Please Kim, I-I-m sorry, you have my word that if you just let me go, there will be no retaliation against you. I swear! All the money you desire as well! ANYTHING YOU WANT, I SWEAR TO YOU!!!"

"Lux, your word means about as much as a hill of beans right now. I am going to kill you now. It is nothing personal, really. I enjoy killing. After all, isn't that why you had originally hired me to do? I just want you to get your money's worth, is all. Now feel free to scream and beg all you like, because that shit turns me on. But make no mistake about it, I'm going to hack you into pieces."

He says something else as I swing the machete down onto his outstretched hand. The blade makes a loud THWACK sound as it digs deeply into the meat of his left hand between the middle and the ring finger. With my foot against his chest, I wrenched it out of his hand, raised the tool and brought it down hard again. This time, I severed his left hand off at the wrist, leaving a jagged hole that spewed blood. I grabbed Lux by his legs and drug him into the middle of the room, so that he was lying on his backside. He was shivering and mewling like a newborn as I began hacking into his left leg with glee. Sweat was running freely down my face. This was quite the workout, better than that insanity shit any old day!

It took ten good swings to separate Lux's left leg from his torso. I grabbed the appendage and flung it away and immediately started on disarticulating his right leg. *TWACK-TWACK-TWACK* went the blade as I savagely cut into his quadriceps with genuine pleasure until I separated that appendage from his dying form. Lux's screams had taken on a watery gurgle, like I submerged him under water. His face also had taken on a ghastly white hue. He was nearly as white as a piece of copy paper. But he was still alive, and that was all that mattered.

Again, the machete blade fell in rapid succession on his left arm as I lopped it off. My arm was feeling fatigued, but I was in a frenzy, so I pushed that feeling away and focused on the carnage at hand. Sinew barely connected his left arm to his torso, so I grabbed it and began twisting and yanking it like an overzealous dog with their favorite chew toy. With one final massive tug, Lux's mangled left arm tore away from its socket with a loud popping sound. Bone marrow intermingled with blood poured out of the grisly hole I just created.

Miraculously, the old bastard was still kicking, albeit just barely. His blood languidly flowed from his countless wounds, and his sounds reduced to moans and garbles. With my forearm, I wiped the sweat from my brow and began savagely hacking off his last remaining appendage, desperately wanting to sever it before he died. The blade continuously crashed onto his humerus, first cracking the major bone, then pulverizing it completely with my savage hacks. After the destruction of his bone, the arm quickly cut away with only a few extra swings.

I watch, enraptured, as Lux's mouth still gasped for air. Shit, this is one tough, old bird! That left me one last option: decapitation. I grabbed the archaic prick by his hips and pulled him closer to me. I placed my foot on his chest so I can keep him right where I wanted him. For a moment, we both look into one another's eyes. Mine are hate-filled while his are terror-stricken. A single, large tear plummets down his face. I grin and hack into his throat, severing his jugular immediately. The lack of blood flow is anti-climactic, though, as it only spurts a small freshet of plasma onto the ground.

Unperturbed, I continue to hack into his supple throat until I can lift his severed head to my own. Lux's eyes have rolled into the back of his skull, only leaving the whites exposed. With one last act of savagery, I smash his head into the wall until the top of his skull cracks apart like an egg. His brain matter coats the side of his head and my hands as it slides down from the horrifying wound I created.

I drop his head and immediately kick it far down the corridor like I was playing kickball as a child. It rolls haphazardly for a moment before crashing into the far wall with a wholly satisfying crash. This has been a delicious appetizer to be sure, but now I am ready for the main course. I am ready to finish Morticia once and for all.

"Ready or not, here I come, bitch!" I say, laughing hysterically as I walk out into the refreshingly chilly night and begin stalking my prey like a slasher movie villain.

Chapter Twelve

Judith To The Rescue

It was such a lovely evening that I decided to fart around outside and just get a break from being cooped up in my room constantly. It had been excessively hot and nearly unbearable for months, but tonight was the first real break in the weather. A cold front had come through and dropped the temperature over twenty degrees. It felt wonderful outside. I watched the fleeting, misty cloud puff from my mouth because of the chill in the air. I have just been reading on my kindle and vaping some potent weed I got from my friend, Lindz Cook, the other day.

I was about halfway through the new Ottessa Moshfegh book, Lapvona, lost in her amazing verbiage, when I was startled out of my reverie by an injured woman falling in front of my house with a sickening thud. I quickly got to my feet and ran down to check on her.

She moaned in pain when I turned her over to see what was wrong. It did not take a doctor to see that a large caliber gun had shot her in her shoulder blade. She also had various scrapes and bruises all over her ivory skin. She gave off a very gothic girl vibe. From her almost luminescent skin tone to her jet-black Bettie Page haircut. She also was wearing a t-shirt depicting the cover artwork for Chandler Morrison's book Dead Inside, a favorite of mine. I am pretty emo myself. I mean, what teenager isn't right?

One of my favorite movie quotes is "*Dear Diary: my teen angst bullshit now has a body count.*" it is cliché as fuck but I don't care. Damn, I love Heathers, the original, not that dreadful remake. I snap back to reality and ask her.

"Hey lady, are you, like... okay?"

She groans like an un-oiled wooden door might, and looks at me with obvious pain in her eyes, accompanied by a wry smile.

"Well, let us see, I've been shot, beaten up, lost my best friend and I am probably being hunted by my serial killer of a nemesis as we speak. I would say I am doing, like, totally the opposite of okay."

Damn, the sass on this chick was on my level. I like her already! I look around the desolate street, fear suddenly gripping me in a stranglehold. Did she say a crazed serial killer was hunting her down? Fuck that!

"We must get you off the street. I will take you into my room, and we can hide out there till the coast is clear. My name is Judith Sonnet, by the way. What is your name?"

"My name is Morticia, Morticia Maggot. I would say you do not have to do this, but without your help, I am as good as dead. I am afraid I need you, Judith. After all that she has stripped away from me, I cannot allow that crazy bitch to win."

I look at her and see the pleading hope in her blood-shot eyes. It only takes a moment to make my decision. I want to help Morticia. I felt a kind of kinship almost the moment we met. The idea of just leaving her out here to die a horrible death is just too monstrous to fathom. I put her good arm around my shoulder and heft her up slowly as not to hurt her too badly. I slowly help her into the back of my house and up to my bedroom so my family does not see what I am doing. They would be livid if they knew I was putting my whole family's lives in danger for a stranger.

It was a risk for sure, but my analytical mind won out. I mean, how on earth could this crazed lunatic know where Morticia went or who helped her? Once I got her safely into my bed and addressed her wound by cleaning it up the best I could, I bandaged it up. Morticia then filled me in on her incredible story, filling me in on everything that had transpired before our lives miraculously crossed paths. I sat beside her, totally enraptured by this incredible and intense story. After she finishes her tale, I just sit there in stunned silence.

"I feel like I just heard the craziest story ever! Wilder than A Serbian Film and Martyrs combined girl!"

"Ah, a true horror fan! Now imagine living this shit, girl. It blows fat dicks."

"Someone should turn it into a damned book. I bet it would be the most extreme thing out there, period!"

"Nobody would believe any of this happened in real life. Now, if someone wrote it as fiction, then maybe." Morticia says with a tired grin.

"I think I might try to rest my eyes for a bit, Judith. You don't mind, do you, hon?"

"Rest a bit M, I will keep watch for you, although I am sure we are golden like Ponyboy."

Morticia grins from my Outsiders reference, even though it pains her to do so. A slight cut on her face opens from the act of smiling, and a small blood trail trickles down to her chin. She absentmindedly wipes it away and lays down on my rat's nest of a bed and almost immediately falls asleep. Her soft snoring is the only sound in my room. I bounce downstairs and check on my parents who are busy watching tv together.

   I go to the fridge and grab a Coke Zero and head back upstairs. My older brother, Dakota, looks like he is playing his video games online as per usual. His headphones are on, so he doesn't notice me standing in his doorway. I walk to the next room where my ten-year-old little brother Connor is reading a dog-eared copy of Alvin Schwartz's Scary Stories To Tell In The Dark. He looks up at me briefly and gives me a wan smile before diving back into his book.

   I smile back at him and leave him to his spooky little tales. I look outside the window and survey the neighborhood. It is like it always is; silent as a graveyard. Satisfied that nothing bad is going to happen, I light-heartedly stroll back to my room with a smile.

Chapter Thirteen

Homing In

As I continue my journey to find her, at a breakneck pace, I get a whiff of her sent yet again lingering in the air. Her scent and something else. It is her... blood! This distresses me to no end. She is obviously hurt and I need to go even faster than I am now. I am exhausted, but the thought of her pain drives me onward. The only positive is that I am infinitely closer to her now. Her scent is much more prevailing now.

I am making a lot of headway, but it does not feel fast enough. Her life depends on me finding her. This is an absolute fact and I can feel it in my core. I propel myself into the night faster than I thought possible. I am almost there; I keep saying it to myself like a mantra. I only hope I can make it in time now.

Chapter Fourteen

Follow The Bloody Breadcrumbs

I STAND OUTSIDE THE makeshift escape route created by Lurch and view my immediate surroundings. It leads to a filthy alleyway with only one way to go, so I follow it out into the desolate streets. I look around and sigh. This is going to be like finding a needle in a fucking haystack. It is like a ghost town out here. I briefly flirt with the idea of just saying fuck it and going on my merry way and getting on with my life before this bitch rudely interrupted it by inundating herself back into it, but I can't. I need to avenge my brother's death. I am not letting her get away with this.

I should have killed her when we were teens in school, but after the maggots in the bucket prank, the bitch totally disappeared from the planet, thus vanishing her from my thoughts as well. She was always nothing to me, anyway. A harmless bit of fun to distract myself from the banality of school. My disdain for her was only because she fought so fiercely against the norm. Even though I felt like an entirely different entity than all my cohorts. I knew I was a wolf in sheep's clothing nearly all my life, but I played the role of your typical well-adjusted teen girl because *I... desperately... wanted... to...fit...in...*

But in my private life, I was far from normal. Abnormal was a more appropriate mantle. My home life mainly comprised of watching real gore videos and torturing and killing small animals for pleasure and posting them on the dark web for zoo sadism fetishists everywhere. I even once took a power drill and shoved the 8-inch bit up a little puppy's anus, turned it on and jumbled up its intestines like swiss cheese while topless, just to make some money, and satisfy my growing bloodlust, of course.

I eventually graduated to killing humans and never looked back since. Humans die better than animals. You can relate to their pain and they are articulate. A squawking puppy makes the same sound regardless of me squashing it in a pair of stilettos or not letting the damned thing out of its kennel.

Even after all these years, my one genuine regret was never killing Morticia Maggot. Life teaches the cruelest lessons sometimes. I chickened out, killing her when I had the chance. She would sometimes go for long walks on a very desolate trail. I could have easily hidden in the foliage till she walked past me and caved in her skull with a rock. It would have been easy to make it look like a rape gone wrong type of scenario. But no, I was frightened of the concept of murdering a person back then, and because of my cowardice, my brother died horribly at her vile hands.

But this time, I will not fail in snuffing her out. I have come too far now. I will not stop till her light fades from her eyes with these two hands. I desperately search for clues to discover where this bitch absconded to, when I finally see fresh blood droplets on the street. It must be from her gunshot wound!

I got you now, cunt! I follow the bloody breadcrumbs down the street to her still secret hiding spot. I get to the end of the street and follow the blood trail as it appears to lead down the sidewalk to a neighborhood a few 100 yards down the street from where I am right now. It must be where she was headed, as it is the only foreseeable house that appears to be inhabited in this crummy area. I quickly run down the street and arrive at my destination. It leads to a big, two-story, slightly rundown home. I glance at the grass and see a larger pool of blood, like she had stopped here for a bit of a respite, or passed out momentarily. I follow the trail further up into the yard where the droplets appear once again.

I sneak up and investigate the window and peep a pair of middle-aged, dumpy-looking people watching television, zoned out like a couple of zombies. It is a man and a woman, presumably the oblivious parents of whoever helped Morticia try to make a clean getaway from me. I stare at them while they mindlessly shovel popcorn down their gullets like cows grazing out in a field. I step away and make a trek around the house to see if anyone else is downstairs besides the two grazers in the front.

Once I arrive back at my starting point, it is clear that everyone else is probably upstairs, which is the way I want it. I feel like Michael Myers creeping around outside, and Morticia is my Jamie Lee Curtis. But the bad guy wins in my movie, bitch. I head to the back door and test the knob, but it's locked, which is no big thing since it has a glass front. I quickly and efficiently break the glass and reach my hand inside to unlock the door.

The two watching tv must be nearly deaf because the program they are watching is on full blast, easily masking my intrusion into their home. I enter the darkened kitchen and quickly scan my surroundings until I find what I am looking for. I rustle through their knife drawer till I find what I am seeking; a razor-sharp butcher's knife. It gleams like a beacon in the night, as it reflects my demonic stare on the stainless-steel blade. I cannot wait to use it on that emo whore and her new butt-buddy upstairs.

My bloodlust is churning right now as I head to the staircase and begin to ascend the steps. Upstairs, I hear an amalgamation of sounds. I hear a young child reading a spooky story to himself. *The Babysitter,* by the sound of it, if I recall. I hear music softly playing and I hear an older sounding male cussing and playing what sounds like one of those military shooter video games. Everyone is in their own little world as the Grim Reaper edges closer and closer.

I am about to crush their little worlds, and it excites me greatly. My wrath has been building nonstop since this whole fiasco started. Nothing, of course, went as planned, much like life itself. But when life gives you lemons, make some lemonade with it, I say! I, of course, have always rolled with the punches in order to reach my endgame; the unfathomable death of Morticia, and here we are. She is so close to my grasp now. I go to the room at the end of the hall, the only one I have not checked yet. I peer into the slightly ajar old wooden door.

I see a cute teen girl on her phone sitting at her desk. Her walls are adorned with various horror movie posters. Some I know, others are more obscure to me. I have never heard of a film called *Anthropophagus*, but the image of the man on the front devouring his own intestines is quite jarring. I make a mental note to myself to check it out. But all of that is quickly forgotten when I look at the bed. Like a bloody version of Sleeping Beauty herself, I see Morticia, clearly in dreamland without a care in the world, for a little longer at least. I momentarily think of bursting through the door with the element of surprise, but their yells would surely rouse everyone up at once, thus making my job infinitely harder.

Then an epiphany strikes me. I will use her love for her family against her. I creep back down to where the little boy was reading his book and enter his room like an apparition. He does not even realize I am in there with him. It is not till I am directly behind him, placing the icy blade of the butcher's knife against his little throat, making him briefly yelp in fright.

"Make another sound brat and it will be your last!" I hiss into his ear.

"Nod if you understand, little piggy."

He desperately nods his head to appease me, his new master and leader.

He cries almost inaudibly, and pisses his little Spider-Man pajama bottoms. What a disgusting little fucker. That is why I never want kids. To me, they are nothing more than revolting parasites. I am going to have a blast slaughtering this little brat in front of his shocked family when the time is right. I tell the little piggy to come with me. We are going to go get his big bro and then go see his sister.

He momentarily hesitates when I tell him to go, so I savagely grab his little throat and throttle him on the floor until he becomes a blueish hue. I viciously lift him back up and tell him to get his ass in gear or I will kill him right now.

He nods vigorously, and we march to the next room. I stand in the doorway, the little piggy in front of me, the knife in front of the little piggy's throat. A thin trail of blood descends to the collar of his t-shirt. I sway slowly back and forth continuously, causing the teen to glance up from his game. It was quite humorous watching his expression change from confusion to utter fear.

"What the actual fuck?" the teen says.

"Get your Poindexter ass up, punk, or I will gut this little kid like a fish right here in front of you. Do you understand me?"

His face turns ashen, and he visibly gulps while nodding furiously. Just to prove I am not fucking around, I push the blade just enough to penetrate the little piggy's chubby little cheek. Blood blooms like a beautiful flower from the gash and trickles down his pained, terrified face.

"Stop lady, I will do whatever you say alright, just don't hurt my little brother!"

"Then get up and do exactly as I say! Let's go visit that sister of yours and get in on all of this fun we are having!"

I tell him to get in front of me and the little piggy and don't try anything stupid or I will fuck him in his asshole with this butcher's knife. He visibly winces from the mental picture and hops right fucking to it!

We file in a single line and walk down the hallway to the last piece of my home invasion puzzle. The older brother stops at the door. I guess honoring his sister's privacy. How fucking chivalrous! I give him a curt nod to go in, which he reluctantly does. Almost immediately, I hear the girl chastise him for abruptly entering her domicile without permission until she sees me marching in with her little brother at knifepoint.

"Oh my God, what is going on?" she says in a quavering voice.

"You have something I want, and I have something you want. I am going to tell you this one time. We are going to be quiet as a pack of little mice while we head downstairs to visit your parents. We are just going to join them and watch some tv, no big deal really. But let me stress one thing. Anyone who tries to make a ruckus to let your mom and pop know that something is rotten in Denmark and I am going to cut off this little boy's head and make his older bro fuck the ragged stump, am I making myself crystal fucking clear?"

I see a bevy of furiously nodding heads, which causes me to inwardly snicker. Everyone in this house will soon be dead. Horrifically, and violently killed by these two skilled hands. It is funny how the human brain will stubbornly cling to hope in the face of utter hopelessness. It's one of the worst of all the human traits people have. I am just thankful I lost my humanity a long time ago, freeing me from all these worthless, earthly constrictions.

"Now, grab that unconscious cunt on the bed and let us get this shit-show on the road. What's your name, gamer boy?"

"Dakota, ma'am."

"And what's your name, girlie?"

"Judith."

"Alright, Dakota and Judith, heft that bitch up and get her downstairs. Any tomfoolery and baby bro here is maggot food. No pun intended to that passed out twat on the bed."

They both reluctantly nod in agreement, and commence to getting Morticia on her unsteady feet. She is still out of it, which is fine with me. I would prefer to get her wrapped up like a present and downstairs before she regains consciousness fully. She may be wounded, but she certainly will not be a pushover. Nothing is more unpredictable or dangerous than a cornered, frightened animal.

We form a figurative human centipede and head down the stairs towards the front room. It does not take much to get the parents in line and docile once we arrive. I stab Dakota in his gut, in a totally non-lethal way, to get my point across, which goes over extremely well, if I say so myself. With Judith's forced assistance, we tie everyone up with some rope she found in the adjoining garage. I put Morticia and the parents on the couch, next Dakota goes into the recliner.

I make Judith grab a chair from the dining room and then I tie her to it next, extremely tight just to make her suffer more. I can already see the rope biting into her soft skin, welting it up almost immediately as she cries quietly.

"Make this a lesson to yourself Judith, keep your nose out of other people's business. Just think, if you would have followed that cardinal rule, I would not be preparing to slaughter your entire family right now."

The mere mention of a mass slaughter sends the family into hysterics. Their wails of grief and sheer terror are nothing more than music to my ears now.

"Feel free to scream. This area looked like a literal ghost-town outside. Here, I will even help you, HELP! OH MY GOD, SOMEBODY FUCKING HELP US! POLICE! BATMAN! SUPERMAN! HHHHHHEEEEEL-LLLLLLPPPPPPP!!!!!"

That shuts their yaps up with a quickness. Now they see just who the fuck they are dealing with. A natural born killer.

I walk around and make sure there is no chance of someone squirming out of their restraints and try to rain on my parade. After some thorough investigation, I decide that Houdini himself could not escape this shit. I walk up to Morticia and begin slapping her as hard as I can until I eventual rouse her from la-la land. Her eyes are momentarily swimming around in her skull until she sees me in front of her. Immediately, her body becomes rigid as she bucks against her restraints.

Corded veins appear on her forearms and on her neck as she rages against her shackles. It is almost admirable. I lower my face to hers and look her dead in her feral eyes and tell her. "I got you now, bitch. How about we play a game?"

Chapter Fifteen

Heaven's Biggest Angel

I'S FINISH GOING THROUGH the white light tunnel, and end up at the giant gates of Heaven! I mean, its gotta be, right? It's like we are on top of the cloud's jus' like I thought it would be like as a youngin'. When I get to the gates, they magically open for me, so I mosey on through.

For a moment, I am a mite afraid. At first, I don't see a soul. I holler out in hopes it rustles up somebody, anyone! I's scared like a hapless goon to be all alone after gettin' kilt by that no good varmint Miss Kim. I get ready to holler again when I sees someone headin' my way. I can tell it looks like an old codger, but that is it at first.

He walks slowly my way and as he gets closer, I get a feelin' of recognition. It looks like my dear ole grandpappy! But that can't be, he died up in Cowgill years ago of old age! Like a kid at Christmas time, I holler out in joy.

"GRANDPAPPY, IS THAT YOU???"

"Well, if it isn't my wonderful grandson, git over here, boy, and give your Grandpappy some neck sugar!"

Neck sugar is what we's call it when he kisses on my neck and tickles me with his neck whiskers. I've missed that somethin' fierce! We hug tighter than two bugs in a rug and smile at one another. It's like some kinda wonderful dream that I's don't wanna wake from! I watch all the tears on my Grandpappy's face and I start to tear up myself. I look at my Grandpappy standin' and it's like I finally remember that he was a cripple when he was alive, so I's asks him.

"Grandpappy, how'd you get yer legs back?"

Well, sonny, when you die and enter the pearly gates, it's like a do-over, I suppose you could say. When I passed away, I jus' was able to walk again. I feel dandy to boot as well. Nothin' ails me no more."

I's thinks to myself that this is a dadgum miracle! Here I am in Heaven with my wonderful grandpappy and he's got his legs back! I kin now see tons of folk walking' on the clouds, jaw-flappin' with one another, not a care in the world! It is a picture perfect day, not a cloud in the purty blue sky. I suspect ain't no cloudy days in Heaven, no siree bob! I's thinking all these thoughts in my noggin when Grandpappy snaps me out of my thoughts and asks me a question.

"I'm awfully sorry ya got kilt, boy. I saw it all happen up here. We have means to keep an eye on our loved ones, yes we do! Who was that woman that kilt ya, boy? She seemed tough as all get out!"

"Yeah, I got murdered by a no-good, cantankerous cuss of a woman named Miss Kim White, for tryin' to protect my best friend, Miss Morticia. We got ourselves in a heap o' trouble and I's got stabbed to death and ended up here in heaven wit ya Grandpappy."

"That's a damn shame, sonny boy. But if it makes ya feel better, your gal pal looks to be joinin' ya soon, I might reckon'."

I's stop dead in my tracks and look sternly at my grandpappy and ask him point blank.

"How do you know she's about to die?"

"Well sonny, I jus tolt ya! Turn them dadgummed ears on! When you get to Heaven and become an angel, you're able to keep tabs on yer kin. You can look down to Earth and see exactly what's goin' on down there, kinda like magic. That's how I knew to meet you at them their pearly gates, ya see?"

"Can ya show me how to do that, please?"

"Sure thing, sonny. Ya jus' shut yer eyes and concentrate real hard on the person you wanna see and then ya will see 'em!"

I close my eyes and concentrate jus' like he says to. I picture Miss Morticia's purty smile and think of all of our good times and it makes me wanna cry! Then I see that rotten Miss Kim, and she has a bunch a folk tied up around her in a house I's never seen before. All the folk look real scared, especially Miss Morticia cuz Miss Kim ain't even givin' her a chance ta fight fair! It's a bunch of shit if ya ask me! I snap myself outta the vision and holler like I's a crazy feller.

"Grandpappy, I's gots ta help my friend! I love her, and she needs me to help her. Miss Kim is gonna butcher her like a dadgum hog or a deer. I can't let that happen!"

"Settle down, boy, don't get yer dander up! It can't be helped. You up here and she's down yonder on Earth. This is what the Lord calls the circle o' life, I suppose."

I's start feelin' like a rabid dog or somethin'! I start pacin' round like a loony bird, mumblin' to myself and throwin' a dadgum fit like a lil' kid. I's start hollerin' at the top of my voice and commence ta poundin' on my noggin cuz my inner voice is tellin' me this is ALL MY FAULT! I's fall to my knees and start blubberin', jus' knowin' that Miss Kim is gunna torture Miss Mortica so bad fore she kicks the damn bucket. I's 'preciative I's made it ta Heaven and all, but even if I 's gots ta sell my soul to the Devil ta go save my buddy, thens I's gotta do it! I's gets up offa the ground and look at my Grandpappy with tears fallin' and dripping downs my face and tells him what I's gotta do now.

"I's gots to go back Grandpappy, Maybe I's should talk to God or even the Devil and try to strike up some kinda deal or somethin'."

"Boy. I's gonna whip the tar outta you if you bring up the Devil here in Heaven!! Quit bein' so damned blasphemous!"

"I's don't care. Imma go try to jaw flap with Satan right now!"

Grandpappy runs up to me and clamps his hand over my damn yapper. He looks spooked, glancing round like he is about to tell a tall-tale or fib or somethin' and says.

"Look, boy, I need you to settle down a hair. Last thing I need is the Lord to show up and hear you jibberin' about selling yer soul or somethin' ridiculous like that! Now listen up. When yer grandpappy first came to Heaven, God had heard about my special moonshine even way up here. He begged me to make him my special batch of shine and even said he would grant me one wish if I made it for 'em. Now, of course, I's did it, sheeiiit, he's the dadgummed Lord and savior for Christ's sake! Now I reckon I's could give my wish to ya on account that yer my boy an all, plus I's loves ya wit all my damn heart and I's hate to see you hurtin'."

He gives me an awfully powerful bear hug, which shocks the hell outta me since back on Earth he was feeble as all get out! He seemed as strong as me now! But I's can tell that he is tearin' up whiles he is huggin' me. So I's start crying too. I's just got here, to my dear ole Grandpappy, and I's already trying to leave 'em. But this is important work I's gotta do. I's let her down once, and that's one too many damned times, I say!

"Thanks, Grandpappy, for givin' me yer special wish. Will I ever git to see you again?"

"Why sure Sonny! Ya got to Heaven once, didn't ya? I suppose as long as you don't act a dang fool, you'll come back again one day. Now don't cha head back down there and immediately git yerself kilt right away. I jus' got the one wish!"

"I won't, Grandpappy, Imma be real careful this time!"

'Good to hear, boy! Now, whenever you're ready, jus' shut yer eyes and concentrate on exactly where you want to be and the process will begin. Don't go thinking it's instantaneous or somethin'. It's a process from what I've heard. You jus' keep picturing where you want to be and it'll work, my boy. I loves ya."

I look up to tell him I loves him too, but I's all alone again. I suppose I got to concentrate for this to work so he skedaddled on me. I's gets down on my knees and begin to think of where I wanna go. I picture it in my noggin' Miss Morticia in that house an' keep repeating the thought like a skipping record. I pray as hard as I can and hope to Hell I won't be too late this time...

Chapter Sixteen

Homing In Part 2

I CAN FEEL A shift in the air suddenly as her body dumps an overabundance of endorphins, which I can only assume is because she is in great danger! Her scent permeates the air so strongly that it almost makes me dizzy. I am so close; I can feel it in my entire being.

I am so tired though! But I get the distinct feeling that her life will depend on me making it in time, so with maximal effort, I zoom off with exponential speed and an almost manic sense of purpose. Her life depends on it and I cannot let her down!

Chapter Seventeen

Crushing The Little Piggy

I WAKE UP TO find myself staring face to face at Kim... Fucking... White. Oh yeah, I am also tied up, and not half-assed tied up either. This is master level knots right here! This crazy bitch really took her time on me! I look around the room and see Judith staring at me wide-eyed in fear. I absolutely hate that I got her in hot water for being a good person and helping me out.

I look around the room and survey the other captive people. Great, two parents an older brother and a little fucking kid. And Kim over here looking like the Grim Reaper with titties. No Lurch to bail me out either. I have never felt more hopeless in my entire life. I am Jack's utter dejection. Kim looks at me with a maleficent grin plastered on her face and says matter-of-factly,

"I will celebrate your death, bitch!"

I could try and say a witty quip, or zing her crazy ass, but I am in no way ready to kick the hornets' nest just yet. One wrong move or sassy comment will get my ass killed quicker than you can say *REDRUM*! I feel like we are all only moments away from being the fourth entry of the August Underground film series. What the fuck am I going to do? Kim begins pacing around the room, stopping by each little fly caught in her spider's web, smiling like the cat who ate the canary.

"Alright class, time for roll-call!" Kim announces to us.

"Let us see, we have Morticia, Judith, Dakota, Little Connor, whom I decided to re-name little piggy because, why the fuck not? And last, but certainly not least, we have Al and Peggy. A regular fuckin' Brady Bunch. Let me tell you guys something. I am so looking forward to brutally murdering everyone in this room. Morticia, I am saving your bitch ass for last. And believe you me, girl, it is going to hurt bad. We are talking next level torture for your ass, girl!"

Great, I think to myself. Kill me already! I say nothing, though, because I am up shit creek, and your girl doesn't even have a paddle! I guess one positive is she is going to kill me last, which bides me some time to think or to weasel out of these restraints. Kim stares at me expectantly as I look up. She has that devilish gleam in her eyes, so I know whatever it is she is about to say is not going to be good.

"So, Morticia, since you took it upon yourself to come into these innocent people's lives, I think it is only fair that you get to pick the order of their deaths, don't you? I mean, their lives would be just peachy keen if you did not ruin it, just like you ruin everyone's life you come across. Lurch is dead, and it is your fault, after all."

Hearing that cunt utter my sweet boy's name lights a fire up under my ass, but I am not stupid. She is trying to get my goat and make me do something stupid, but I am not stupid. When I get the chance, I am going to eat that smug cunt's *face off* like I was the John Woo flick.

"You want me to pick someone? Sure, I can do that. Let us go with Little Connor, I guess." I say nonchalantly.

All the family audibly groans, and Peggy blubbers and protests to Kim with a very palpable urgency.

"Please, not my baby boy, he is only ten years old... Kill me instead, I beg you!" Peggy screeches manically as tears drop from her reddened eyes.

"If I get loose, I will kill you with my bare hands, you damned lunatic!" Al rages in his binds helplessly.

"Oh, really?" Kim smugly retorts.

She strides right up to the big man, causing him to cringe in his seat, and takes an enormous bite out of his right cheek like it was a juicy, delicious Fuji apple.

"GGGGGGAAAAAAHHHHHHH" Al unintelligibly hollers.

She stands directly in front of him and chews up his cheek and swallows it and makes a smacking sound after. Her eyes bore into Al's. He shuts the fuck up with a quickness. All of his bravado has poured out of him just like the blood from his cheek wound is doing right now.

"Now, does anyone else have anything to say about Morticia's choice? Speak now or forever hold your peace. Nothing? Good. Alright, Little Piggy, Aunt Kim has a surprise for you!"

She walks over to the little child tied to his miniature chair, bound up tight like a mummy. It didn't really matter; Connor barely had the strength to pop a balloon. His eyes were wide like an anime character's. They also were red from his incessant crying. Kim picked the kid up to her chest and dropped him to the ground hard so that he was lying flat on his stomach. To keep him from squirming away, she put her left foot on top of his back and looked at everyone with a sardonic smile and asked.

"Has anyone here ever seen a crush video before? No? why am I not surprised? Ok, a crush or stomping video is where you walk on an infant or small child and slowly break their bones and cause massive internal damage, killing them. I used to post and upload videos of these that I have done to various children on the dark web. They eventually ended up on some gore mixtapes such as Amber Alert, Suffer the Little Children and Weather Warning, not to mention other hard-core websites. Too bad I can't film little piggy here, though."

I watch in rapt fascination as Kim removes her shoes and socks, so that she is barefoot, for better traction. For added effect, she pops her toes rapidly. After that, the room falls as silent as a morgue. Everyone, myself included, looks at Kim with bated breath for what is next. She slowly walks on Connor's feet and ankles and stops momentarily, prolonging the child's discomfort before the real agony begins. She slowly begins walking up the boy's legs and then abruptly stops, her grin as wide as an exposed skull. She spins in place like a ballerina, crushing his legs. The small bones make a wholly jarring, crackling sound. It is very loud.

"MOMMY! HELP ME, IT HURTS! IT HURTS, IT HU-UUUURRRRTTTTSSSSS!!!!!""

The child screams like a hot poker is being jammed deep inside of him. Kim is now at the youngster's back, and that's where things get really spicy. Once Kim reaches his back, Connor wails from her weight, crushing down on him. I can hear his back creak and groan in protest, like an old house settling. For added cruelty, Kim jumps up and down on his back twice for good measure. A fine mist of blood sprays out of his mouth as he yowls in obvious anguish.

Once she gets to his neck, she puts both feet on the tender area and freezes there like a statue. I can see her weight compress his small, fragile neck, effectively cutting off his breathing passageway, sending him into hyperventilation mode due to fear. His breathing is severely compromised now. We watch as he struggles with all his tiny might to breathe. He starts to turn blue before Kim giggles like a schoolgirl embarrassed about her crush (no pun intended) and continues to ascend upwards to the kid's cranium.

Almost immediately when Kim steps on Kenny's little head, one of his minuscule orbs shoots out of its socket with the force of a bullet. The ropy stalks still tethered to the now excommunicated eyeball. Blood slowly bubbles out like a tipped over ketchup bottle. The child screams uncontrollably as Kim's weight crushes the entire left side of his head like it was made of something inconsequential and brittle.

For the coup de grâce, Kim jumps up and down repeatedly on the poor boy's cranium until his tiny head breaks open like an over-ripe melon, vomiting its grisly contents onto the filthy carpeted floor. The boy's mouth gasps grotesquely in a death spasm as a gush of almost black blood pours out of his deflated head. Have you ever heard a small child's skull split apart? It is a fucking gruesome sound, let me tell you!

Everyone except Kim and I are screaming in shell-shocked horror at little Connor's gruesome demise. I am indifferent, but Kim looks to be in total ecstasy as she continues mashing the child's head into a soupy paste of gore. They are all screaming, but Kim is laughing.

Chapter Eighteen

Momma Bear

PEG LOOKS LIKE A war vet with PTSD afterwards; she has that thousand-yard stare going on and seems totally oblivious to her surroundings. Kim is talking to her, but she doesn't even notice. Until Kim snaps the right arm of the dead, little Connor, snapping the bone like kindling in a roaring fire and snapping the grieving mother out of her fugue state.

"Why do you have to keep on killing him?" Peg wails in unadulterated anguish. Kim ignores the question and instead asks one of her own to the pallid woman.

"Hey, momma bear, what did you think of me popping little piggy's head like a fucking zit? Pretty fucking hot, huh? Hey, want to taste your little boy's blood and brains, bitch? I bet you do!"

And with that, Kim shoves her gore-covered feet into Peg's pale, shocked face, painting her son's gooey viscera all over her visage like a young girl trying to apply her mother's makeup chaotically. Peg wails like a siren once she realizes that bits of her son's brain and bone got coated all over her face like the greasepaint on a clown's grinning mug. To add insult to injury, Kim grabs a heaping scoop of Connor's splattered brains and shoves it directly into Peg's pie-hole, shutting off her gobbles and moans almost at once. Kim clamps her hand over the middle-aged woman's nose and mouth, causing her to ingest her boy's brain tissue.

"Yummy, yummy, get your son in your tummy!" Kim exclaims with real fervor.

And I thought I was an evil she-bitch from Hell, but this gal done snatched the fucking crown! Regina George 2022 Mean Girl of the year right here! I stare at Judith and wordlessly mouth that I am sorry to her. I mean, it is tough for me to feel remorse for humans even though technically I am one. I do feel for this girl, though. She stuck her neck out for me and unfortunately, she is learning an uber painful lesson. It was a something I learned a long time ago. It is the opposite of Nike's famous slogan. *Just don't do it* is my motto. Trust me, you will thank me later. Judith gives me a sad nod; I suppose resignation set in for her long before her baby brother got stomped into oblivion like splattered roadkill. Her brother Dakota is obviously seething in his seat. He looks like he wants to rip Kim to pieces with his bare hands. Trust me, kid, I can totally relate. That is my hopes by the end of this whole fiasco as well. Judith stares at Kim balefully, tears streaming down her face like a waterfall.

"Why are you doing this? You have Morticia now. Why are you still hurting my family?"

Kim stares at the teen girl long and hard, almost like she is calculating an exceptionally hard equation, before she speaks to Judith.

"Why you ask? Well, it is rather simple honey, you stuck your nose where it did not belong and for that, I must teach you a lesson. And that lesson is the boogeyman is real, and you have found her."

She grabs Judith by her lips and gives it a brief but savage squeeze before she saunters off into the kitchen and pilfers through the various drawers as she searches for something, a weapon I would wager. She comes back to us, arms behind her back like she is about to give us a wonderful present. Wonderful to her, at least, since the present is almost certainly a painful death. She glides effortlessly over to Mama Bear, allowing me to see what is in her hand; an old timey meat tenderizer. Kim bows down, so that she is forehead to forehead with Peg, causing the middle-aged woman to recoil and flinch in terror from her proximity.

"Are you ready to join your little piggy, Mama Bear? Because I can totally, like, make that happen for you right now. Just say the words and I will sever your ties with this world so you can join your brat in Hell."

I stare in awe as I watch Peg look at Kim, then turn her haggard gaze down at the pile of desecrated flesh on the ground that once was her living little bundle of joy. I watch her chin tremble uncontrollably and the tears welling up in her eyes. She nods furiously as the waterworks carpet her flushed face. Kim unveils the weapon from behind her back and brandishes it menacingly at the older woman. Both Dakota and Judith plea with her to stay strong and that they love her. Al looks totally catatonic right now, oblivious to what is about to transpire. With a wholly terrifying war cry shocking everyone, Kim brings the meat tenderizer crashing down on the top of Mama Bear's skull, making a distinct cracking sound. Almost immediately after, a steady stream of blood runs down from the top of her wounded head and runs down into the woman's right eye, coating it completely. She makes a sound reminiscent of a cow giving birth, bleats, and moans spurt from her esophagus like a vomitus meal. Kim strikes her face this time, knocking her bloodied right eye deep back down into its socket, like a squirrel tunneling an acorn deep into its nest. Mama bear looks absolutely ghastly, a new empty eye socket crying tears of blood down her cheek. It also appears that her upper cheek bone is broken from the thunderous hit as well. She is now making this creepy and annoying sound that I wish would just stop.

"E-E-E-E-E-E-E-E-E-E-E-E!!!" Mama bear keeps caterwauling like a siren.

"Shut the fuck up, you annoying cunt." Kim says.

She then gives her a massive strike to her mouth, shattering her teeth, sending them clattering everywhere, including down her throat, finally shutting her the fuck up. Thank God, if I was not tied up, I would have belted that cooze across her face myself. I watch as Mama Bear's head droops down, oozing a combination of blood, drool, and teeth that steadily begin pooling into her lap and making a small moat of ichor.

Kim lifts her head back up by wrapping her hair in her fist until she is drunkenly looking up at Kim as if she was wishing on a star. Kim then continually strikes her face with the tenderizer, leaving its telltale crisscross design peppered all over her fractured and crumbling face. The sounds of breaking bone fill the air with their abrasive percussive melody. A musical for psychopaths, if you will. Kim then lets loose of her inner barbarian and pounds her head into rubble, leaping around her, jackal-like, literally foaming at the mouth. The strikes to her annihilated head sound jarring and appalling all at once. Mama Bear's pate collapses upon itself, her skull no longer having its form from the constant barrage of strikes it has had to endure.

  Kim begins to relentlessly hammer down onto her forehead with a seemingly limitless fountain of energy and vigor. It is very fucking impressive. Finally, her head cleaves apart, blood sprays in twin brownish geysers, staining her already admittedly disgusting top. It is accompanied by an atrocious hissing noise coming from the wounds in Momma Bear's skull, places where bone and flesh no longer are connected as they once were. She bears a striking resemblance now to a Jackson Pollock painting; all splashy, drippy, and especially messy. Really fucking messy.

Chapter Nineteen

The GoodFather

DAKOTA AND JUDITH VIOLENTLY gag in unison at the sight of their mother's violent demise. Dakota vomits on himself, leftover spaghetti by the looks of it, onto his Lorna Shore band T-shirt. Judith is rocking back and forth and mumbling to herself. She has already seen two family members violently and cruelly dispatched by an all-too dangerous psychopath. Two down, three more to go. Kim stoically stares at all of us. I would have better luck trying to read a mannequin's face right now. She is giving absolutely nothing away.

I feel like she is saving me for last, so I am good, but the others? Anyone could go at any second by the looks of things. Kim looks at Judith for a moment, and I can see the wretched cogs in her brain concocting something repulsive to do next. She looks from Judith to Al before she announces to everyone in unison.

"Hey Judith, do you think your dad and brother want to fuck you? After all, you are really fucking cute, if I say so myself. Play your cards right and maybe I will scissor you later!"

I stare at Al and Dakota and watch their faces blossom red with embarrassment. Jesus, is Kim going to take this scenario where I think it is headed? Obviously, this bitch is totally vacant in the morals and soul department. I guess some people have a real sick idea of entertainment.

"What do you say Al, want to get your dick wet inside of your little girl's cunt?"

The words are like weapons to Al's ears. He flinches like they are punches to his face, sinking him back into the recliner like it was swallowing him like a sentient being.

"How dare you say something like that, you lunatic! Of course I don't want to do that to my little princess!"

"The lady doth protest too much, methinks."

Kim giggles maniacally in Al's petrified face. She ruffles the flustered father's hair playfully, then sets her sights back on Judith and asks in a sugar sweet, sing-song voice.

"How about you Judith, wanna see your daddy's dick? Wanna put it in your mouth? Or how about your pussy? I bet you fantasize about it, you little slut."

She playfully slaps Judith in the face and even pinches her nose like one would do to a child. Judith is in full-blown ugly cry mode now and quietly, almost inaudibly, says through shuddering gasps,

"You are a monster; I wish I could get loose and kill you."

"Bitch please, you kill me in a dream. You better wake up and apologize. I do the killing; your kind does the dying. I am an apex predator all-fucking-day-long-bitch!"

Kim's hate filled gaze now lasers back onto Dakota. Her mischievous smile re-appears as she asks him,

"Dakota, you are awfully silent!" She chirps brightly. "You ever sneak a peek at your sis getting out of the shower? I bet you have! Maybe you even drilled a hole into her wall so you can spy on her. Men are all the same, after all. Walking hard-ons, controlled by their little heads."

Dakota begins to squirm in his chair. It could be discomfort, but I get the sneaking suspicion that there is some truth to what Kim is saying. A broken clock is right twice a day, you know? The kid looks like an incel, so it does not shock me that he might sexualize his sister in some way. I mean, hentai can only get you so far, right? An epiphany appears to strike Kim, and she runs back into the kitchen, furiously digging in the drawers for something. With a flourish, she raises the item into the sky like the sword of Excalibur or something. That item is a glistening pair of poultry shears. They are designed to be able to cut through bone, chicken skin, and other tough materials. This does not bode well for my little friend, I suppose.

Kim treads directly to Judith and quickly cuts off all her clothes with the shears, leaving her as nude as the day she was born. Al quickly looks at me almost at once. I guess he is not a pervy dad after all. But interestingly, Dakota does not look away. His eyes swallow her visage whole, like an alcoholic finally getting a much-needed cocktail. I can visibly see his dick getting hard as a rock. Well, this is going to be fascinating, I think to myself. Kim looks at Dakota with a knowing smirk, and walks over to him and quickly and efficiently pulls down his gym shorts and underwear, freeing his raging hard on.

"Woah Nelly, now that's a fucking boner!" Kim says. "It looks like you have a big, and I do mean big, fan over here, Judith!"

Kim puts her hand around the young man's above average prick and gives it a few tugs, causing Dakota to moan slightly. Judith looks at me and visibly gulps in equal measures of fear and revulsion. I think she is just now realizing where this shit-show is heading; Incestville, population 2.

"Kim, is all this insanity necessary, girl? I mean, if you are that fuckin' horny, go hop on Pornhub and rub one out. Trust us, we will wait."

"Morticia my sweet, unless you want me to go over there and cut out your tongue, I suggest you shut up and just be glad that I am saving you for last. So, sit back and enjoy the show."

Well, I never was one to stick my neck out for another human, but I tried for Judith. I mean, if these ropes weren't tied so fucking professionally, I could have escaped and killed this malodorous bitch already, but apparently, she was a damned Girl Scout in her youth or something. I still am hopelessly tied up, and I have tried my best to loosen these binds the entire time. Kim was going to say something else lurid, I am sure, when Al interrupts. He implores her with tears streaming down his weathered old face.

"What if you can kill me as slowly as you want? Will you just leave my little girl alone with all this sick sex shit? I know you are going to kill her no matter what, but I beg you, please do not make her go through with this AND then kill her as well."

Damn, look at Dad of the year over here, very noble of you, pops, AND very stupid. I guarantee Kim will take you up on the offer! I look to Kim, who is looking at Al with that cocked head thing like Jason Voorhees or Michael Myers, which is almost never a good thing.

"I like your style Al, you got yourself a deal. Now let us give the audience what they came for, carnage candy! You look like a handy guy. Do you have a workbench where you keep tools or something, super dad?"

"Y-y-y-yes, it is through that door in the garage."

"Wonderful. Let me look through there and see if I can rustle me up a fun way to dispatch you pops! Now do not go anywhere, I will be right back!"

And with that, she runs off in the garage's direction. God only knows what she is going to come up with next. Hopelessly tied in place, we wait for our inevitable demises in quiet melancholia.

Chapter Twenty

Batter Up

It is funny how time can get away from a person, you know? But I think Bender said it best when he expounded, "*There's nothing to do when you're locked in a vacancy.*" I fucking love *The Breakfast Club*! I feel like I have been tied up for days, but it has only been mere hours. I know one thing, though; my ass is so fucking numb from this hard as fuck chair right now. I look to Al, and the big sweetie is shushing Judith and telling her how much he loves her and tells her that everything is going to be okay. It is a lie we willingly tell ourselves, of course, but right now it feels nice to pretend that we all are not about to be massacred by this fruit loop nutcase. I look and see that Dakota is still eye-fucking Judith, and his pecker is still as hard as granite. Did he eat a bowl full of Cialis tonight or what? I mean, damn! I look at Al, still trying to soothe his daughter, but it is obvious he is getting sick of his son's lecherous stares at his sister.

"Son, what the fuck is wrong with you? She is your blood, not some random girl on the street. Get yourself under control, for God's sake!"

"I can't help it dad, it's like my ultimate fetish." Blushes Dakota.

"You mean to tell me you are into this incest shit, boy?"

Dakota stays mute, but his silence says more about the subject than any words possibly could.

"I feel like we're trapped in this sick degenerate's mind!" Wails Judith.

"More like a couple of sicko's minds, it would seem." I say off-handedly.

"Stop trying to humiliate me!" Fumes Dakota brattily. "That's called kink shaming, and it is NOT okay!"

"Boy, shut the fuck up with that nonsense." Al grumbles menacingly.

After this ultra-stimulating conversation, everyone shuts their traps, enveloping us in a fog of awkward silence and glum. The only sounds now are from Kim rustling around in the garage. I am about to ask Judith something when the garage door opens with panache, banging into the wall and leaving an indention from the doorknob. Kim waltzes in brandishing her new toy; a Louisville Slugger tightly wrapped with barbed wire. This bitch is more black-hearted than I ever thought possible. I mean, sure, I knew she was an extreme cunt in school, but this is ridiculous. I have known some real American Psychos in my time, namely Pat Bale, but if he ever had a dark twin, she would be it. Both are the devil incarnate. I truly believe that. Kim walks right up to Al, who is absolutely pissing his pants right about now and asks him.

"Are you ready for your unfathomable death, daddy?"

"Y-y-y-you promise afterwards you won't try that weirdo-kinky shit with my baby girl, right?"

"You have my word, pops. I will not let your weirdo, incest-loving dork of a son plunder your baby girl's pussy, Scout's honor," Kim even throws up the hand sign to boot.

After saying that to Al, she quickly looks at Dakota and gives him a mischievous wink, which causes Dakota to beam brighter than a thousand-watt bulb. So much for honor among psychos, I guess. Luckily, Al does not seem to notice this. The last thing he needs to worry about before she brutally murders him is whether this psycho whore is an Honest Injun, for Pete's sake.

"Now it is time for you to for you to keep up with your end of the bargain pops, are you ready for what I got planned for you?"

Al does not speak to Kim, but he does nod his head in agreement at her. He looks at Judith and they both share a quiet, bittersweet moment together. Judith mouths I love you and Al reciprocates and gives her a little wink. They both are crying silently. If I was a normal human being, I am sure that this would be very moving. I am Jack's total lack of empathy.

"I am sure you are familiar with the gangster movie *Casino*, right? The one where Joe Pesci gets beat to death with a baseball bat and buried in the desert while he is still alive. Well, guess what pappa? We aren't doing that! Instead, I am going to take this bat wrapped in all this beautiful razor wire and I am going to anally rape you with it. That sounds like sexy fun, right? I know it is already making me want to cream my jeans!"

Damn, that is some cold-blooded shit right there. Everyone is staring at Kim like they are not sure they heard her correctly except me. I know what the bitch is capable of. Shit, it sounds like something I would come up with! Once the weight of her words sinks in, Judith sobs in great big gasps and Al is trembling as if he is in a blizzard without a coat. Dakota is still just staring at

Judith's tits and pussy in equal measures, little head in total control, while his big head is totally shut off for the time being.

"Alright Al, I am going to help you up so we can remove those pesky sweatpants of yours. I need to see what I am working with."

She brusquely lifts Al up and coldly yanks down his pants clinically and efficiently, leaving him exposed to us and ashamed. She looks at his genitals like she is conducting a science experiment, giving it a curt nod, as if in approval.

"Nice schlong you got there Daddy-O, you sure you don't want to stick it in your daughter's hole instead of taking your medicine?" She brandishes the deadly bat to drive her point home.

"I would rather die than defile my girl, you sick, demented psychopath."

"All good things come to those who wait, Al my sweet. Trust me, the anticipation is my aphrodisiac. It is like a drug to me, the prolonging of sweet, sweet suffering. I am going to make you suffer soooo good, baby!"

She roughly shoves Al over the side of his recliner so that his old man, pancake ass is skyward, giving us all a bird eye view of his hairy brown eye. She has him positioned like one would do to a child that they are about to whip the hell out of for not doing their chores. Judith, of course, is cringing in anticipation of watching her dad die in front of her, but me, I am engrossed in excitement. Watching the human body go through extreme suffering is, like, my jam.

"Now Al, I know you probably expect me to try to just force this into your man-pussy with no lube, but I am not that inconsiderate. As a matter of fact, I am going to use one of the best lubricants there are, which is, of course, blood. Now, small amounts of blood will not work because of coagulation. It will just get all tacky, which simply will not do! But a lot of blood? Now we are talking. Then it is like the consistency of motor oil. I should be able to fuck you nice and good with my new toy, then. All we must do is a little foreplay to get the blood flowing on you."

   I watch in absolute fascination as this agent of chaos goes to work on Al's midsection with the deadly bat, swatting at his midsection, rending sections of his love handles to ribbons. The steady *THWACKING* sound of the bat solidly striking human tissue, ripping it as easily as one would shred a newspaper. I watch as flecks of meat float through the air like grisly dust particles. The blood blooms out from the gashes like a rose growing out of a crack on the sidewalk. It is a thing of beauty in all this depravity. Al's moans and cries of pain sound more like white noise to my ears, like he is a million miles from me right now. I cannot focus on much besides the beautiful blood right now. Judith is crying next to me, begging for Kim to stop hurting her father. It all sounds like buzzing flies to me.

   Thinking of buzzing flies transports me back to the day I was laying hip deep in a dilapidated garbage dumpster, stuffing my eager beaver with maggot riddled rotten meat that was left to putrefy in the sun for days on end. That was the first time I almost died from my impure proclivity to self-harming myself. I vigorously shake my head, trying to dispel this weird mental fog that has enveloped my thoughts. Is this me seeing my life pass before my eyes because I will be dead soon? *Snap out of it, bitch*, I think to myself over and over until the volume around me gets turned back to acceptable levels again.

When I come back to reality, Judith is still screaming for Kim to stop hurting Al. Al is draped over the chair still, only now he is a bloody mess. The exertion his body just endured has him sweating like a racehorse after winning a race, soaking the chair in his perspiration. Dakota is till ogling his sister's breasts and licking his lips. Kim, of course, is soaking the bat in Al's plasma, as well as spooning handfuls of his blood and coating it around his anal cavity.

"Okay Al, pucker up buttercup. Let us do some deep mining, eh?"

For a moment, I think Al has passed away because of his silence. That is, until the head of the bat slowly enters his puckered asshole, almost as stealthy as a cat burglar. Then it is like a switch is flipped, bringing him instantly to life and screaming like nothing I have ever heard before in my life. His voice goes up two whole octaves by the sound of it. He bucks frantically, like a steed trying to dislodge a cruel rider who will not stop kicking it with their piercing spurs. I stare elatedly as she fucks his ass frantically like an overzealous lover. Every time Kim pulls the bat out before re-entry, it reminds me of a plumber snaking a toilet; desperately trying to get it unclogged. Only now what is being excised is not just shit, although there is a lot of it, as well. Tendrils of intestine, intermingled with chunks of bloody meat and unknowable body parts, fall out of his ruined orifice, plopping around his feet, all the while Kim hums a tune, *The Sign*, by Ace of Base, if I am not mistaken. I love that damn song, such a bop!

Kim continues her blasphemous rape of Al, the teeth of the razor wire destroying everything it meets with total ferocity. His cavity becomes cavernous as the weapon tears and expands his ruined hole to astounding levels. It looks like you could stick an entire human's head into that hideous hole now. Kim continues her sexually mutilation on Al, sending the bat so deep into his ruined and gutted asshole that every time she removes it from his gaping sphincter it fountains out a massive blood-shit-gore diarrhea concoction, carpeting the floor with its abhorrent contents. Both of his interior and exterior sphincter are torn asunder, and his rectum is hopelessly tangled to the razor coated bat, causing it to pull out after every vicious pump from Kim. It is apparent that Kim is beating a dead horse, or raping it, I mean. Clearly, Al has passed away. There are no more guttural yelps of pain or jittering movements from his anal evisceration.

Kim removes the gore-caked bat like Excalibur being expelled from its entrapment in the stone, thrusting it into the air in celebration, sending cascading droplets of blood on her like a gentle spring rain, before tossing it to the ground reminiscent of a victorious Spartan. Kim turns to the captive audience and stares at us like we are specimens in a zoo.

"I know I promised Al that I would not allow Dakota to deflower his own sister. I mean, I am sure he is an honorable man that would never welsh on a promise; but I... have... been... known... to."

Chapter Twenty-One

The Incest Chapter

KIM WALKED AROUND THE room, surveying the absolute damage and misery she has heaped upon this family like a drill sergeant inspecting a new recruit's bed-making abilities, or lack thereof, at boot camp. I fidgeted around in my seat in discomfort; I was fighting a losing battle not to piss myself; I felt bloated, like a young bird. Kim regards me with derision and a soulless stare.

"Why are you flopping around like you're having a seizure over here?"

I stare directly into her hate-filled eyes and shrug the best I can in my restraints.

"You would look like you are mimicking Michael J. Fox too, if your back teeth were floating like mine are right now!"

"You think I care if you piss yourself, you dirty goth-cunt? I am not your trailer trash, momma. You can soil yourself all day long for all I care."

I did not even waste my breath with a rebuttal now. When I get loose from my restraints, I will get my pound of flesh out of her ass, and that is a fucking promise. I am Jack's all-encompassing rage. Kim turns and walks over to Dakota, obviously bored with me and my overflowing bladder issues. If I can hold it long enough, maybe I can piss down her throat and drown her like a sewer rat in a bucket. I watched Dakota blatantly ogle Kim with obvious lust. She gave him a knowing, mischievous wink.

"What are thinking about handsome?"

Dakota blushed furiously but meets her eyes and responds,

"I want to fuck my sister right now!"

Judith cringes back into her seat like she had been assaulted with a fetid stench. Kim, on the other hand, snickers loudly and retorts,

"Damn Dakota, that sounds fucking hot. You are kind of getting me wet with how pervy you are. I like it."

And with that, she slides her hand down between Dakota's legs and begins to lightly stroke his rigid cock, squeezing the head until a glob of pre-cum drools out from his dick slit. Kim then uses the human lube to pump his schlong to full attention. She then demurely gets down on her knees and nuzzles his cock against her lips at first, then sucks gingerly on the head ever so slightly as she playfully jiggles his gonads. I watch Dakota stare up at the ceiling before closing his eyes and moaning in total rapture.

I felt my pussy get all dewy, like on a Sunday morning as well. Hey, what can I say, you guys know I am a degenerate! I gaze away from the budding fornication going on and let my regard fall upon Judith. She is still blotchy-faced and hiccupping gasps of breath from watching most of her family get brutally massacred in front of her very eyes. Eyes that are still shedding bountiful tears, but she is also gawking at Kim play the ole skin flute on her brother.

I take a glance at her nude form and even though she has seen absolute Hell tonight, her body is reacting to the sexual stimuli. I see her nipples are as hard as little pebbles from the constant dumping of oxytocin in her system. She looks ashamed, but she is stimulated none the less by their foreplay. I can also see a smattering of vaginal transudate leaking from her quim. It is obvious she is sexually excited, hence the arousal fluid discharging from her swelling clam from the increased blood flow. Does Judith secretly want her brother's bone or Kim's cunt? Damn, she is a little pervy minx after all! She finally notices me rubbernecking her and looks at me abashed.

"What is going on over there, girlie?" I ask her.

"Uh, I don't know, Morticia," Judith says while blushing furiously. "I guess I want to feel something other than fear and terror right now. Kim is going to make me fuck Dakota no matter what, right?"

I wordlessly nod in silent agreement at her.

"I mean, I am probably going to die tonight and I have not even gotten the chance to live my life yet. No sex, no drugs, nothing. Just one big, boring, introverted existence. Maybe if I act like I am really into it, she will lose interest in the whole pervy-fuck-my-brother-incest deal, right?"

Or she might just slaughter you instantly, I think to myself. I kind of figured this whole turned on sis routine might have just been a ploy, and I was correct. I must give it to her for shooting her shot at least.

"Yeah, maybe so Judith. I guess what those old fucks say about nothing ventured, nothing gained, must have at least some credibility."

She nodded in agreement, her face lit up from the possibility of alluding to not only fucking her sleazoid brother but also surviving this night from hell. *Fat chance, you silly ditz,* I think darkly to myself. I knew Kim as a teen, not so much this relentless killing machine she has become. But I have a sneaking suspension that the bitch is going to shit a bunch of fucking bricks when Judith tries to flip the script on her. Then she will take said bricks and bash her brains out all over the floor!

Almost as if the mere thought of Kim in both of our thoughts manifested some sort of triple mind-meld, Kim abruptly stops sucking Dakota's meat missile with an audible pop; reminiscent of opening a new bottle of wine for a celebration. She then scrutinizes us like the lead detective in a major crime case. We both gulp in unison from her flinty glower. She rises from her kneeling position in front of Dakota and drunkenly uses her forearm to wipe the excess fluids from her grimace plastered face.

"What are you two etiquette crotches blathering about?" Kim says, suspiciously eyeing us both warily.

"I was just telling Morticia that the thought of my bro's penis going up inside me really has me sprung right about now!"

Kim stared intently at Judith like one would gape at watching 2 Girls 1 Cup for the first time. She looks disgusted that it was not only HER idea now. Hell, even Dakota seemed like he was fighting a mental fugue, for fuck's sake! Everyone was having a brain tumor for breakfast with a side of hash browns, it would seem.

"So let me get this straight, Judith, just so everyone is crystal clear. You are ready for your brother to use and abuse your nubile, young body, correct?"

"Absolutely Kim! The sight of you going down on Dakota has got me wetter than a slip-n-slide!"

Kim visibly drew back from that statement like she had just been struck particularly hard in the face. I could see the mental duress she was under momentarily. A true intellectual quandary if there ever was one. Then, almost like magic, her cock-sure smirk re-appeared on her bitchy face. She looked at Judith pityingly and slowly shook her head back and forth.

"Nah, I think we are going to call an audible on this play coach." Kim says coldly. "They are trying to blitz us on third and long, it would seem."

Another sports analogy? I inwardly cringe at the utter audacity of this. Sports talk sounds like a lot of clicks and whistles to this here gothic queen. Somebody shut this autistic cunt up already! Dakota, could you please stick that juicy wang of yours back into that psycho whore's soup cooler's again??? All joking aside, she seems irate at this turn of events, until an epiphany strikes her viciously and unceremoniously.

"Hold that thought Judith, I got something that can get this night back on track and make it eXXXtra spicy!" Kim says and runs off back to Al's garage. Great. *This is fucking ominous,* I think. We are in a dour situation for sure, but Judith seems at ease. She cannot be this gullible, right? Kim returns with a flourish, hand ridiculously hidden behind her back, like a bashful child. She even is lightly pawing the ground with the tip of her shoe, like an antsy boy asking the girl of his dreams out to dinner or a movie before finally talking.

"So, do you remember earlier when I mentioned possibly scissoring you? I would really love to do that to you right now. You could say that I have an appetite for your destruction right fucking now."

And with that, she brings her arms out from behind her. Gripped tightly in her fists, are a massive pair of gardening shears. Who does this bitch think she is? Cropsey from The Burning? I watch as Judith's eyes expand to the size of frisbees. She stares at Kim in absorbed terror at what she is implying. It went over her head at first, but it quickly circled back though. *Attention passengers, we have just lost cabin pressure*, I think to myself.

"What do you say, Judith? Let's scissor baby!" Kim says caustically with a venomous smirk.

Chapter Twenty-Two

Scissor Me Timbers

JUDITH VISIBLY GULPS IN absolute terror, recoiling violently from the gardening shears being thrust into her shocked face. She instinctively sunk into her chair as far as her body would allow, which was not very much at all.

"Kim, I don't understand. I am totally willing to fuck and suck Dakota. Isn't that what you wanted?" Judith cawed in befuddlement.

"Exactly twat, what I wanted. Now that you want it, it no longer titillates me. You seem to have forgotten a very fundamental fact, silly little girl, and that is I am running this monkey-show. So instead of a sex show, we are going to continue making a death show instead!"

"Woah Kim, wait a sec!" Dakota chimed in quickly. "I thought you said I was going to get to fuck Judith. How can I fuck her if she is dead? "

"Jeez, dummy, ain't you ever heard of necrophilia?"

"You mean sex with a corpse?" Dakota asked doubtfully.

"Duh."

"What is so cool about porking a cadaver?"

"Get a clue, bone-head." Kim sneered. "Not only can you fuck your sis' cold, dead pussy, but you can also desecrate her body. Cut her head off, bite off her nipples, stick my barbed wire bat into her cunt, whatever you want."

Dakota's eyes sparkle as he considers the myriad atrocities he could bestow on her once she no longer was among the living. I can see his dick twitching in eagerness. And I thought I was fucked up! Judith bleats in fear like a wounded lamb after hearing the new game plan. Kim creepy crawls her way right up to Judith and rubs her clitoris in earnest. She does that for a bit before switching it up and inserting two digits knuckle deep into the girls' dripping and juicy box. Judith, obviously in the throes of ecstasy, closes her eyes and thrusts her drooling clam savagely against Kim's probing fingers. I look at the bitch as she quickly darts out her tongue and flicks it against her saturated cunt.

Kim carpet munches the shit out of Judith, allowing her hands the freedom to grasp the menacing garden shears. As Kim continues to lap at Judith's sex like an overly zealous dog, she raises the weapon like an archeologist might raise an artifact to a crowd of onlookers. She positioned it right at the precipice of her pussy. And right before Kim uses the shears, she ferociously sank her teeth into Judith's swollen clitoris, mashing it to a pulp with her incisors before viciously biting and tearing at it like a puppy with a new chew toy. Kim's head brutishly shakes back and forth as the tissue begins to raggedly tear free from Judith's pubis.

Precious life-fluid begins to lightly spray a fine, pink mist as Kim's commanding teeth untethered the blood-engorged clitty with a wholly satisfyingly snapping sound; the final sinews snapping loose from all the savage butchery being thrown at it. Judith's howls of agony are quickly eclipsed to an even shriller octave as Kim pushes the bottom blade into her gooey joy-trail, leaving the other blade clamped down unceremoniously on her crotch region. With both hands gripping the handles tightly, her knuckles turn white. Kim squeezes the handles together and cuts Judith's cunt apart. Continuing a swath of destruction upwards, Kim continues to cut into Judith's malleable, tender flesh. Judith screams in white, hot agony, corded veins pulsing visibly from her neck as she hollers in agony, bug-eyed and writhing like an ant being burned with a magnifying glass by an evil child.

Kim viciously hacks and cuts at Judith's mid-section, flaps of skin separate, showing the jaundiced pigmented yellow fatty tissue below the epidermis. Tendrils of intestine poke their head out of the newly made cavity like a cautious, nosy neighbor. I look at Judith's pain wracked face. Her nose is producing non-stop bloody snot bubbles from all her hyperventilating. They burst all over her face and begin again like a time loop. Blood steadily streams from her mouth, making her teeth turn a ghastly crimson as she shakes her head like a wet dog, sending her fluids cascading all over the room. I think Kim must have fallen off the rails because next thing you know, I see her stuff her face deep into the gouged crotch, feasting on the gristle that hangs morbidly from Judith's shredded and ruined cunt. The bodily destruction, as well as vulgar molestation, is appalling, but Dakota and I cannot look away.

I think about how this pretty young girl, whose entire life was still ahead of her only hours ago, tried to help me out. The cost of my life was hers, and it still looks like I will be up for the slab soon enough. So, what was the point of all of this? If this is what you get for sticking your neck out for someone, it is why I never bother with humanity, except when I slaughter them, of course. I have not felt bad for a death until recently. First my poor dear Lurch and now Judith. I must be getting soft in my old age! Is it any wonder why my outer shell is kept impenetrable in the first place? Feeling human hurts! That is why I walk the path of an inhuman monster in the first place. I have been an outcast my entire life. Is it any wonder why I cast out and reject humanity? Deep thoughts by Morticia Maggot, right? I cannot help it, though; this has been the most traumatic moment in my entire life, and it still is not even close to being over.

   I snap out of my reverie to see Kim has stopped using the scissors. She is now extracting Judith's entrails from her brand new, gaping maw of a pussy with the same delight a child would have on Christmas morning. Judith moans softly as her head awkwardly rests against her heaving chest. Her body shivers from being on the brink of death, her arms are both etched in goose-flesh. Once Kim has most of her intestines pulled out and snaked around the floor, she grabs a handful of the innards, wrapping it tightly around Judith's neck and chokes her with her own guts! Her eyes pop open in astonishment, her pupils dilating from the sudden lack of oxygen to her suffocating lungs. Kim gazes into Judith's unblinking, watery eyes, with her own blazing optics.

   "Thought you could pull a fast one over me, didn't you, little cunt? But guess what? You do not have the intestinal fortitude! Consider this an homage to your favorite horror film!"

   And with that, Kim constricts the viscous innards even more tightly around the girl's crushed windpipe, squeezing until her tongue lolls out, and her eyes turned red from all the broken capillaries. Mercifully, Judith's neck breaks from Kim's wringing of it with her own organs. It sounds as if someone broke a good-sized stick against their knee. Judith's body immediately plummets to the ground afterwards, thudding heavily. Her body jittered from the collision, shooting blood out of her slaughtered, ruined womb, carpeting the floor in bloody chunks. The grisly scissors still cruelly jammed deep inside of her drooling sex. Kim turns back to her final two captives, me, and dipshit over there, and drinks us in with her hateful regard.

"Alright Dakota, how about you get over here and start fornicating with this gutted bitch?"

"I guess getting a piece of my dead sister is better than nothing at all!"

Chapter Twenty-Three

Molesting The Cadaver

DAKOTA IS VISIBLY BUZZING with excitement as Kim escorts him to his dead sister's ruined form. He went from a smiling creepo into a frowning creepo in two shakes of a jackrabbit's ass though once he peered at her now quite literal axe-wound. Yikes, and that pussy now looks grizzlier than Grizzly Addams ever did! Kim stares at Dakota as she watches his face droop worse than my neighbor's after his stroke. She looks like she wants to kick his ass all the way to next week over his pouting. I mean, we all know guys are nothing but big ole babies, so I am not sure what her damage is. Dakota better look out though, bare minimum, best-case scenario he is in for the biggest ass chewing of his life. Worst case? He will be nothing more than human hamburger by the end of this fucking shitshow.

"Why are you looking so glum, chum?" Kim asks.

"Well, I really wanted to fuck her pussy, but it is like, you know, totally obliterated and shit."

"So, you are such an incel simp that you didn't know women had other orifices you can stick your dick into?"

"Well, her mouth would be boring, and well, I have never used the, uh, Hershey Highway before."

"Yeah, and actually using the phrase *Hershey Highway* will probably ensure you will never get to find out."

To that attack to his fragile ego, Dakota clamped his mouth shut, but shot her a blazing glare, after Kim had turned around, of course. She had once again plucked up the gardening shears and turned to face the awkward teen weirdo.

"Dakota, my sweet, I am going to create a whole new, extra special pussy hole just for your pussy ass!"

With three quick paces, Kim was already standing next to Judith's corpse. She raises the sharp blades of the shears to Judith's near-translucent ghost nipples, and in one efficient snap, lops off her left nipple with the ease of slicing into warm butter..

"What-did-you-do-that-for?" screeched Dakota.

"Well, it is rather simple, bub, I want you to fuck this supple breast meat right here. I want you to get balls deep inside her mammary glands and pummel it till you full up her mammary glands with your juicy jizz!"

Well, I knew we were in FUBARville, population 2, at this point. I mean, *fuck her titty*? This bitch is a couple of sandwiches short of a picnic. I take a looksee over at incest-boy and see he is looking like the cat who ate the canary. Of course, this sick objectification of women titillated (pun intended!) his incel, black-pilled, loser ass! Kim grabs his cock and puts it in a crushing strangle hold, making the boy yelp out in pain and shock. She positions his dick to the tender, newly uncovered breast meat, and lightly rubs it on the exposed nerves like one would to a clitoris in a Brazzers Video on Pornhub. Kim slowly slobs on Dakota's red, engorged knob for a bit, before shockingly hocking a loogie directly onto Judith's very dead titty with an audible smacking sound.

The noises of her breast meat tearing open as Dakota slowly pushes his oversized phallus deeper into her breast tissue, was not only startling, but left a bitter taste in my mouth as well. Slowly the teen's cock began disappearing deeper into this Frankenstein's monster of a vagina, sending out a jettison of blood onto his pubic hair and balls as he pushed his engorged member inside of her. He furiously begins fucking his corpse-sister's breasticle (I made a new word!) like a character out of a damn Jorg Buttgereit flick. I watch as Dakota is fucking his dead sister's titty with absolute concentration, zeal, but above all else, total mirth.

While all this wicked debauchery is taking shape, Kim has absconded into the garage again, this time re-appearing with a machete from its dark, claustrophobic confines. She watches this incestuous necrophile's antics with a detached, clinical look of interest, like a psychiatrist might garner towards a particularly interesting patient. She had wanted to fuck the young man; I was sure of it. She had a hungry, feral look in her eyes. But if I had to wager on it, she wanted these appetizers to be over already, so she could work on the main course, which is your girl right here!

I was really fretting about my upcoming demise. A part of me always figured I would have gotten loose from my restraints by now, snuck up behind Kim's loopy ass, and broke her neck with a loud snap, like a dry piece of dry kindling to be burned that night on a blazing bonfire. But no, this is not some action movie where the hero saves the day at the end single-handedly against monstrous odds. This is real life. And sometimes real life kills the good guy. Sometimes the ending you deserve is not the fucking ending you get. Life's a gyp sometimes, like when you ordered those Sea Monkeys out of a comic book, thinking it would be this huge underwater race of creatures wearing crowns and shit, and then it is just some fucking brine shrimp that are boring as fuck to watch!

Kim raises the machete as Dakota inches closer to his orgasm; I watch as his rump pumps faster in and out of Judith's used and abused titty tissue, flashing his "O" face in the process, highly flushed and sweating profusely. He looks like fucking Rain Man spazzing out because he is about to miss The People's Court with Judge Wapner! But that is all about to end now. Judith's scumbag of a brother is about to take a dirt nap, which makes me feel... nothing. It will be one less degenerate beta-male in the world, which is truly never a bad thing, though!

Kim is still hesitating her death blow on Dakota, which at first puzzles me quite a bit. Then it hits me like an abusive, drunk step-dad; she is waiting for this freak to unload a copious stream of his baby batter inside her tit-hole! We are then both startled out of our respective revelries by dick-face shouting in rapture to the sky.

"I am getting ready to blast-off! This tit feels better than any pussy hole could I bet! It is so tight, and this fatty tissue slime that is oozing out sure makes fucking it a breeze! YEE-HAW!!!!"

It was obvious he was spasming from one helluva nut. At the exact moment his frenetic humping subsided, the machete swung down with a wholly satisfying *SWOSH-ING* sound, imbedding itself deeply into the meat of Dakota's shoulder blade, nearly tunneling itself into his chest before abruptly stopping to a halt. It happens so fast that at first, the lecherous teen did not even realize he was gravely injured. The last few spurts of his disgusting semen had only just seeped from his gore covered dick, when a massive spray of blood fountained from his chest wound.

He unbelievingly looks at his chest in exaggerated shock and horror before falling on his back with a thud. Kim quickly hops on top of his increasingly bloody form and strikes at his outstretched hands, that are desperately trying to block her ruthless attacks. The sharp blade of the tool made quick work of Dakota's left hand first, efficiently lopping it off at the wrist with little effort. The blood barfed out of the ghastly stump and spewed him and Kim with his vital, life-giving fluids. Dakota half-heartedly tries to block her strikes with his remaining right hand and quickly receives the same outcome. Only now the blood does not jet out as fiercely as before because of the massive blood-loss going on elsewhere.

Without hesitation, Kim quickly shimmies out of her pants and underwear, quickly descending her drenched sex on top of Dakota's still insanely erect cock. She sinks all the way down on the dying teen's massive shaft with an audible grunt of pleasure. She then grinds her pussy against him, gyrating in orgasmic ecstasy while the youth visibly turns pale from the massive blood loss, turning whiter than an archaic dog turd left to molder out in the backyard. Dakota croaks some inarticulate shit at Kim, who in turn puts her pointer finger directly against his lips and mouths the word "*Shhhh*" playfully. She then grabs the machete and slowly and seductively starts sawing through Dakota's pale, outstretched throat.

A bubbly, gurgling sound emanates from his brand-new gaping neck wound as Kim continues riding him, cowgirl style. She continues sawing, going back and forth with the blade, severing his windpipe, causing it to make a hideous, whistling sound. I can tell she is adding tons of torque to her quest to sever his fucking head off. I can see his head has only a little bit of gristle and sinew holding his cranium in place as Kim continues to fuck and cut with an almost blistering pace. Her moans of pleasure blunting out what little squeals of pain Dakota could still muster from his ruined throat. She arches her back as she is rocked with what looks like a one earth shattering orgasm. I can see Dakota's crotch region is covered in fluids; blood and Kim's vaginal discharge glisten in the room's light.

With one final vulgar display of power, Kim brings the machete down, cleaving off the top of Dakota's head, causing his brains to jostle out of his severed brain pan and slide down his cheek, falling silently onto the ground with a faint *plop*. Kim finally wrenches his mangled head loose, snapping its final restraints and brings the disembodied head to her lips, which she hungrily kisses, snaking her tongue into his agape, bloody mouth. She intermingles her very much alive tongue with his very much dead one, sucking on it before carelessly tossing it into the corner wall where it makes a pleasant smacking sound as it collides, even leaving a blood trail in its wake to slowly drip to the floor.

I am thinking this atrocity exhibit must be over, but Kim has one last act of sadism for poor ole Dakota. She hovers above his ragged neck stump and pisses down his stump and into his esophagus with a glib look about her. As if she is trying to say she is the queen of obscene or some trite bullshit like that. I am Jack's total lack of enthrallment. Her apple juice tinted urine spills over his ragged neck stump, cascading down to his messy genital area, mixing with Kim's cunny juice, as well as blood and fragments of brain tissue and skull.

"What do you think of my savage butchery?" Kim asked.

"I have seen waaaay better, if I am to be frank. I killed Pat Bale a million times better than anything you have done so far tonight. You are playing checkers, and bitch, I am playing chess when it comes to brutality. We are not even in the same league!"

Surprisingly, my words cut her deep like a dagger with a jagged edge. She momentarily looks like she is going to cry even, what a loser! Then I see her steely reserve take back over like it never truly went away. She begins to inwardly laugh at first, but soon it turns into a more riotous guffaw that unnerves me. This twat may be crazier than even I thought was possible. We are talking Charlie fucking Manson over here! And just like that, her laughter dies like an aborted fetus at Planned Parenthood.

"Let us just see how much of a basic bitch I am now that it is your turn to feel my wrath, Hot Topic Hood rat. I promise no one will suffer as hard as you are about to. I even brought adrenaline with me to keep that blackened heart of yours pumping till the last possible second."

I look into her eyes and I knew she was dead serious. I was about to be in a world of pain and suffering unlike anything I have ever experienced. I have tried my damnedest to untether myself from these restraints, but the only thing I did was rub my wrists to a goddamned bloody pulp trying to Houdini myself out of this unpleasant quandary. *Are you there God? It's me, Morticia. If you have a Hail Mary type of plan, now might be a good time to use it!*

Chapter Twenty-Four

Deus Ex Machina, Bitches

I FEEL LIKE THAT damn Megadeth song, *Sweating Bullets*, let me tell you! I felt absolutely emasculated by this. My power has been stripped from me at the get-go of this nightmarish night. I guess I can take solace in that, but I am too proud of a girl to let myself be mentally defeated, especially by her. I mean, she made me feel less than for my entire high school experience. And let me tell you, that shit follows you around like a homeless person begging you for spare change! I have a strong façade, to be sure, but I am just a human that has constantly had to deal with the fact that my life is a misery porn on an endless loop. I have built a wall so big around myself that Trump himself would be covetous of that impenetrable shit! Ugh, a political joke? *Bateman must have really run out of ideas, huh? ;)*

Anyway, before I rudely interrupted myself with this mental diarrhea, that is admittedly helping me stave off the reality that I am probably mere moments away from Kim sadistically butchering me like a Cannibal Corpse album cover that never was. I guess I had a good run, right? I did it my way, like I was Frankie Sinatra. I came, I saw, I kicked some ass and chewed bubblegum. But at the end of the day, this she-bitch from Hell is going to let the maggots have their way with me at least one last time.

The only difference is this time I am the meal. I glare at Kim and see that she is absent-mindedly licking her chops like a cartoon villain out of a Hanna Barbera production! She slithers over to me like the snake she is, and gets all up inside my grill, asking me in her bitchiest tone.

"Any last words, cooze?"

"Yeah, try a breath mint."

I feel cooler than Bruce Willis being all defiant in that See You Next Tuesday's stupid face. It was fleeting and bittersweet though, almost immediately after her wounded face blanched from my sudden bravado, she belted me good and hard across my face. Shocking me into silence and neutralizing my smart-ass-mouth like an old battery on a frigid January morning. I feel my cheek welt, and pretend to kill her with my dagger eyes. I would be doing a Dahmer to this obnoxious twat if I was not as helpless as a newborn baby. She stares at me like a glib teacher gloating over thwarting her star pupil in front of a packed classroom.

"Now, do you have any snarkier comments before I murder you? Because trust me, Morticia, I would love to keep smacking the shit out of your *My Chemical*

Romance groupie ass till I knock your clothes backwards like Kris Kross."

I am extremely vexed and out of options right now. I have continuously been trying to free myself on the down low this whole time, quietly trying to break my bound hands free. All it seems that I have accomplished is dug cavernous grooves into my flesh from my restraints. My wrists are killing me and I am probably going to bleed to death. I am no closer to getting loose, no closer to thwarting this heinous cunt. Lurch is dead, Judith is dead, and soon enough, I will be dead.

Kim smiles at me, but her eyes are dead. I am surrounded by death. Normally, it makes me feel secure and alive, but your girl is not quite so used to having the shoe on the other foot. I feel like I'm having a low-grade panic attack because even though I have always flipped the coin like I was Anton Chigurh when it has come to living or dying; I do not have a death wish, far from it. I do not want to call it.

A part of me wants to create something, maybe a book, maybe even a snot-nosed brat to call my own one day. Even though I am death incarnate, I still have this need to nurture just under the surface of my stone-cold killer façade. And this is what is killing me, I have been stripped of my choices by circumstances beyond my control. I am Jack's utter despair. I can hear Kim whistling *Fantastic Voyage* by Coolio as she pilfers in the garage for the perfect tool to fuck my shit up.

"YAY!" Kim squeals in delight.

I guess she has discovered something exquisitely painful for me in there. She walks out of the garage and she is carrying a STIHL brand chainsaw that looks like it has done a lot of pruning in its years. Great, probably means the blade is dull as shit and it will take an extra-long time to dismember me with it. Will the shit-storm ever cease for me?

"Who says you have to be in Texas for a chainsaw massacre?" Kim says with a wry smile etched across her face.

She checks the gas reservoir and nods in approval at the ample amount of gas that is still in the contraption.

"I guess I might start by bisecting your joints at the knee's, maggot girl. But don't worry your pathetic, dyed black head okay? I have tourniquets and adrenaline to keep this going for as long as possible! It will be like the most fun sleepover ever. I will even braid your hair, after I cut off your head, of course."

"I think I would rather take the saw than hear any more of your craptastic jokes."

"Is that so?"

"Yup."

"Where do you want it to penetrate you, tough-girl? The snatch or the brown eye?"

"Gee, they both sound so enticing, I guess surprise me!"

She spits on me like an alpaca. *What a foul bitch, right?*

"I hope this hurts you." Kim mutters angrily.

She hunkers down next to the chainsaw, grasps the pull start and gives it a massive tug, momentarily cranking the small engine to ear-piercing life. Inside the house, the sound is truly deafening. It is short-lived though, and almost immediately after; it conks out. She growls ferociously and yanks the wankie like she is Long Duck Dong. But in all her anger, she keeps forgetting to use the choke mechanism. It is at that exact moment when I hear it. It is a sound that I am all too familiar with. Buzzing. Lots and lots of incessant buzzing. It sounds like a million flies flapping their wings simultaneously. Kim is in the middle of an innumerable number of pulls on the chainsaw cord when she finally hears it too.

We both rubberneck at the side sliding doors, since that is where the sound is coming from, it seems. Our eyes widen in trepidation as we both stare at the glass. At first, it seems to bulge out like a full belly and then forcibly explodes into the room like a chest burster violently burrowing out of its host. A million shards of broken glass hurtle towards the both of us like an army of miniature assassins. We shield our faces, taking the brunt of the cuts to our forearms and hands. Luckily, the damage is only artificial. *What the fuck is happening now? Is this a blessing or a curse for me?*

Chapter Twenty-Five

A Felched Finale

AT FIRST, NOTHING SEEMS to happen. It is as quiet as a cemetery at midnight. Then a huge blur swooshes into the house, blowing our hair all out of whack like a Vidal Sassoon commercial. It then lands directly on the ground in front of us. We stare at it and both recoil in revulsion. It is a fly. But not just any ole' fly. This is the Shetland pony of flies. Oh boy, howdy! Its segmented arms greedily rub its hands together like Scrooge McDuck preparing to swan dive into his gold.

The way its massive compound eyes stare at us, and through us, is some unnerving shit. It looks like it could totally kill us. This monstrosity looks like it weighs 200 pounds. Now I know I have been known to fill my clam with these gross little grubs, but let me tell you. I have never been this unaroused in my entire life. Literal sand box down there right now between my legs.

I suddenly have a sentence ring out into my mind, crystal clear, like someone distinctly talking in my ear.

"MoThEr, I HaVe FoUnD YoU!"

"Wait... I.. am... your... mom???"

"*YeS, yOu BiRtHeD mE iN tHaT cAvE. yOu WeRe TaKeN bY a MaN aNd I wAs LeFt AlOnE.*"

I look at the creature and it nods at me, as if in affirmation. Its robotic voice has a pleasant buzzing sound to it, like somehow it can bend its insect vernacular into human speech. I focus on what I want to say to it and let my mind blast it a thought message back.

"Holy shit, so I really gave birth to you that night in the cave? I thought I was hallucinating!"

"*No MoThEr, It WaS ReAl. I HaVe BeEn SeArChInG FoR YoU EvEr SiNcE We BeCaMe EsTrAnGeD. BuT I NeVeR GaVe Up HoPe. ThEn OnE DaY, I PiCkEd Up YoUr ScEnT AnD I KnEw YoU WeRe In DaNgEr.*" Its weird robotic/insect voice intones.

"Thanks for rescuing me! Do you have a name?" I ask him.

"*No MoThEr, I HaVe BeEn On My OwN sInCe YoU BiRtHeD mE. I HaVe No NaMe.*"

"Hmm, well how about something nauseating like Felch?"

"*It SoUnDs NiCe, WhAt DoEs It MeAn?*"

"It is a freaky sex thing. It means to suck semen out of a sexual partner's vagina or anus."

"*Oh I sEe, I DiD tHaT tO a DeAd WoMaN I FoUnD pArTiAlLy SuBmErGeD iN a CrEeK. I sYpHoNeD iT FrOm HeR pUsSy WiTh My PrObOsCiS. It WaS A dEliGhTfUl TrEaT mOtHeR!*"

"Are you male or female?"

"*I aM a MaLe.*"

I watch as Felch's tongue flicks the air and his head does a complete 360 as he gazes at me and then Kim. I see her continue to recoil in disgust, but I am warming up to the weird little guy. I can only imagine how hard it was for him to find me just by scent alone! I asked for a miracle to save me and someone had to been listening to my pleas. My mind goes back to the night in the cave where I thought I was delusional having a giant maggot baby. I thought it was just a vivid hallucination brought on by the sepsis.

Turns out, only the part where it devoured me was fictional; how sad that my poor son had to somehow fend for himself, but still has risked life and limb to find me even though we were never a part of one another's lives. I am Jack's parental insecurities.

I am expelled from my inner ramblings by the frantic sounds of Kim trying to start up her chainsaw. She looks pallid and sweaty, no doubt in shock by the giant fly boring holes into us both with its huge red eyes.

"This gross thing can eat you alive for all I care, but it is not getting me!" Kim shrieked.

She violently flings the chainsaw into the corner with a guttural roar of displeasure and grabs the machete instead. It was now or never; I was still hopelessly tied to this damn chair and Kim is on the verge of trying to chop up my illegitimate fly child with a machete. We have most unquestionably arrived in the Twilight Zone! With a quick assessment of the situation, I look to my insectile kin and mind-blast him.

"Get this crazy bitch, Felch, or otherwise she will kill the both of us!"

"YeS MoThEr, I WiLl MaKe HeR PaY FoR WhAt ShE HaS DoNe To YoU!"

Ugh, why did I just name my offspring Felch? Fuck it, let us just go with it. I mean if Gwyneth Paltrow can name her little brat after a fucking apple, then why can't I name mine after the sex act of sucking semen out of a partner's anus or vagina right??? Felch springs to action at once, swarming Kim with an almost imperceptible quickness before she can even raise up her machete to strike him. He is upon her, tearing off her clothing with his legs and knocking her to the ground where he nimbly gets on top of her.

"GET THE FUCK OFF OF MEEEEEEEEEEEEEE!!!!!!!!!!!!!!!!!!!!!" Kim shrieks in revulsion mixed with terror. But Felch does not get off her. Instead, a loud gurgling can be heard emanating from his thorax region. Felch lets loose an inundation of his vomit, upchucking it all over Kim's breasts.

His digestive enzymes almost immediately go to work on her mammary glands. The tissue makes a hissing noise from the gush of his toxic barf. Her skin smokes and bubbles as the membrane breaks apart, causing her chest to become concave and causes a massive sink-hole like effect in her chest. A gruel-like concoction seeps into her chest in a viscous muck of melted titty meat, fatty tissue, blood, and liquefying flesh. It looks like some lumpy ass, rancid tapioca pudding after someone squeezed a bunch of ketchup into it. Gross, right?

Now this is where things get mighty gag inducing. If you recall, Kim cannot feel pain. She has what is called Congenital Insensitivity to Pain and Anhydrosis, or CIPA for short. Her pain-sensing nerves are not properly connected in the parts of the brain that receive pain messages. So instead of shrieks of pain, she screeches in disgust as Felch's sights are set on her vaginal area. A stream of drool intermingled with his digestive fluids flows steadily from his mouth and tongue area. Kim beats her fists against Felch's hard-shelled exoskeleton, which seems to have no ill effects on my insect progeny.

"Morticia! Get this monstrosity off me! If you do that, I will let bygones be bygones. What do you say? I mean, it seems fair to me!"

Kim immediately gives me her million-watt smile that she undoubtedly uses on her modeling gigs. I am impressed with her doggedly tough demeanor, but I could see her smile had somewhat curdled in the corners.

"Nah Kim, I don't think I will. You've been a pesky fucking thorn in my side for way too long now. It was not enough that you killed me in high school, not in the physical sense, no, but in all the other important ways you did. You snuffed my flame right the fuck out with a whoosh! Then you killed my sweet, sweet Lurch. A true angel if I ever saw one. A misunderstood giant with a heart of gold, who did what he had to do to get by on this cruel, shitty planet."

"But you did not stop there, did you bitch? Then you had to kill Judith as well. Someone who stuck out their neck to help a fellow outcast in need. She had her whole life ahead of her, but because of one good deed, you slaughtered her entire family. Then you killed her AND then you had her sicko brother molest her cadaver. So, when you ask for clemency after everything you took from us, I say fuck no! Tonight, it seems, the freaks win, not the prom queen. Have at her Felch!"

"YeS MoThEr!" Felch mind-melded in response.

He took another long gaze at Kim's quivering quim before he retched a virtual river of vomitus disgorge and drowned her pussy in its toxic contents with a sound akin to dumping a bowl of spaghetti in a toilet bowl. Kim continues to pummel my offspring, but her wailings became less frenzied and more lackluster in power by the second. Kim has also taken on the hue of a piece of chalk, and was getting paler by the second. Her cunt was sizzling like a grilled cheese sandwich on a skillet and her labia lips were popping like hot grease and turning into a syrupy goop that had the same consistency and color as Rotel dip. Yummy, who has got the chips right???

Kim's ruined cunt looks appalling now, reminding me of that Nazi dude's face that melted in that old Indiana Jones flick. Her pussy has literally turned into a pus-filled porridge, covering the floor as it melts, bubbles and oozes into the carpeting. They are never getting that shit up. Let me tell you! The smell wafting up to me from her beef-stewed pussy hole is feculent. It is truly offensive in every way possible, and I have smelled some repellent odors in my time. I look at Felch with adoration and respect. He fucked my nemesis up. I take a gander at Kim and she looks like someone that did a few rounds with Mike Tyson is his prime. I half expect to see birds and stars literary hovering around her dazed head.

"Hey sweety, want to come over her and help untie your momma?"

"*YeS MoThEr! I aM cOmInG nOw!*" Felch replies in his kooky inflection.

He quickly skuttles over to me and gnaws my restraints loose quicker than you can say, '*savage butchery of an entire family*' and flies back to Kim's shuddering form. I watch with fascination intermingled with trepidation about what was about to happen next. Felch's proboscis emerges from his head as he excitedly hops back and forth in obvious anticipation of what is about to transpire. You see where I am going with this, but I will describe it, anyway. The bug boy's proboscis hungrily dives deeply into the gelatinous muck that was once her vagina. It now resembles beef stroganoff put into a blender on max power for five minutes. Felch happily slurps it right up with his insectile appendage in great big gluttonous gulps and mouthfuls. A smattering of gore mists into the air like dust particles in a sunbeam. Kim's body rocks violently, as if she is currently riding on an extremely rickety roller coaster from his raucous feeding. A smidgeon of blood jettisons from her mouth like drool as she observes her mangled form in apparent awe.

"Am I dreaming right now?" Kim says absentmindedly.

"Why do you ask, because you are dying?" I inquire with elation.

"No, because a giant fly just liquified my tits and pussy and now it is sucking it up like clam chowder through a fucking straw."

"Nope, this is really happening. Say hello to my son Felch."

In response, my fly boy waves to her as he continues to feed on her gooey genital muck. Insanely, Kim waves back, smiling with all the charm of a disfigured prostitute.

"Hi Felch." She says dreamily.

"Man, I did not see my night going this way. I mean, I had your loser ass dead to rights. I was fucking John McClane and your dumb ass was Hans *fucking* Gruber! Now I find out you have a giant, mutant, fly son? Not only that, but he melted my female parts like I was an actress in Street Trash! That was not in the fucking playbook, I would say."

"Yeah, I have a penchant for mutants. I guess the dredges of society are my kin since I have been dealt nothing but countless bad hands of torment my whole life."

Kim looks at me thoughtfully for a moment before she responds.

"Early torment makes torment easily imagined, I think. Go ahead and blame the world for the way your life turned out. It's sure easier than blaming yourself."

I stare at this physical bane of my existence and cannot help but to be flabbergasted by her astute critique of me. I am Jack's reluctant agreement with this disfigured cunt-rag.

"I think you have a good point, Kim, and I agree somewhat with what you have just said. Except that bullying leaves a scar and fills people with a void that can never be filled. I have been an empty shell of myself for as long as I can remember. I have all the characteristics of a human being physically, but on an emotional level, I am nothing but an empty void. A mere specter of my former self. From my rapist and abusive stepfather, to you making me want to commit suicide every day, I never had a chance to be a well-adjusted human. I have only felt like a caged wolf, just waiting to be pounced on and devoured almost my entire life. Well, my mom passed away from morbid obesity, and my stepfather is putrefying in a shallow grave that I planted his ass in many years ago. All that is left now is for you to take a dirt nap. I think I am going to have Felch vomit on your perfect, resting bitch face so he can slurp that up, too. How does that idea grab you?"

I wait for some kind of mean girl, Regina George type of riposte from Kim, but all I get is the sound of Felch slurping up his vagina souffle with all the tenacity of a starving Ethiopian child covered in flies. Finally, she looks unwaveringly into my eyes with a hardness that causes me to involuntarily take a slight step back.

"My brother is gone because of my past mistakes. I accept that now. My wicked life has ensured the karma

I am dealing with right now. I am ready to go now. I... Belong... Dead..."

I silently nod in agreement. She smiles wanly at me and closes her eyes. Her body is almost translucent now, and she is shivering like she is nude in a blizzard. I send a mental blast to Felch to finish her off, just like I had threatened her.

"WoUlDn'T yOu LiKe A tAsTe Of hEr BeFoRe I kIlL hEr?"

"A taste? Sounds kind of gross, but I am a gross bitch. Good idea Felch, let me get a nibble of that crotch stew."

I walk into the kitchen and grab myself a powdered blue Pyrex bowl and a spoon. I then head back over to Kim's hideous, twitching form and kneel beside her. Her pussy porridge is so immense around her once desirable orifice that I can just dip the bowl right into the ruined cavity like it is a ladle. I bring the piping hot vaginal and anal gruel up to my nose and give it a sniff. Hmm, not too shabby. I dip the spoon into the crazy concoction and bring the utensil to my mouth to take a big sip.

The taste is explosive to my tastebuds; causing me to shake my head fiercely, like a dog covered in water. It is very meaty and spicy tasting, like some mad scientist dish from a Mexican restaurant from Hell. My tongue is coated in gruel and I can only assume singed pubic hairs. It is truly nauseating, but the fact that I am ingesting my nemesis is oddly satisfying. I look over at Felch and see him happily drinking the bile out of her pancreas with his appendage with real enthusiasm.

"You taste pretty gross, just so you know, bitch." I say to Kim.

"Did you really think eating human flesh that has been dissolved in fly puke would be a delectable meal, you ludicrous cunt? I hope you get Kuru from eating me and die!" She wheezes like a ninety-year-old grandmother with emphysema.

"Okay, Felch my boy, put this odorous cunt out of her misery!"

"YeS MoThEr!"

He skuttles close to her face and lets out a blast of his foul retching spew once more, engulfing Kim's face in its highly damaging digestive enzymes. I watch her skin blister, redden, and peel. Huge boils appear all over her face as they expand and swell, eventually exploding in an eruption of multicolored rainbow pustules. I watch huge veins form and bulge all over her face like Scanners. The skin bursts from the pressure, spraying blood from the torn flesh skyward.

The gruel cascades down her face in rivulets of ghastly slime. I watch as she opens her eyes, only to have them split in half and pop in her sockets, squirting out onto her cheeks like a half-hearted ejaculation. Their bloody egg yolk consistency slides freely down her cheeks like an emotionally bereft widow. I watch as the acidic belly juice from Felch lays waste to her lips, dissolving the area till only a grisly rictus grin remains. I gape on as the vomitus bile removes most of the outer layer of her face, leaving only the bloody muscle visible underneath. It resembles freshly ground hamburger in appearance.

In the end, all that remains of her once beautiful face was a smoldering, blackened skull with some bits of fatty meat haphazardly left stuck to a few hard-to-reach spots. Felch, being the wonderful meat vacuum he is, snorkels up every morsel with his appendage and sends it into his seemingly never-filling gullet. Boy, can this kid eat or what? Almost as a response, Felch belches loudly, sending vestiges of Kim spraying into the room and landing on me and the tattered remains of poor Judith's ravaged corpse.

Well, this night cannot get any more fucking weird, I think to myself. And just to prove me wrong, at that very moment, I watch the front door explode as Lurch Beauregard himself hurtles himself into the entrance with all his might, smashing it to smithereens! I feel like Arnold from *Different Strokes* hearing some preposterous bullshit and exclaiming in earnest.

"Whatchu talkin' bout, Willis?"

Chapter Twenty-Six

A Family Reunited

I DRUNKENLY WATCH LURCH dust himself off from door remnants from himself. I feel as if I am in a drugged-out daze of biblical proportions. I had watched him die at the very hands of this deceased twat lying here on the ground in a puddle of her own putrefaction. Are we all dead and in limbo or something? I look at Lurch in total bewilderment and timidly wave to him. A lone tear tracks down my eye. *If this is only real*, I think.

He looks at me with tears gushing from his mis-shapen eyes as well, and rushes towards me in a nanosecond, grabs me in those powerful arms of his and mashes me deeply into his chest as he gives me a colossal bear hug! Almost immediately I see Felch go on high alert and fly directly onto Lurch's back and prepare to give him an immense horsefly bite on the back of his neck! I quickly give him a mind blast, trumpeting into his head that Lurch is a friend, alleviating the bug boys' fears. Lurch, on the other hand, looks terrified!

"Jesus H Christ Miss Morticia, what in tarnation is this dad gummed thing?"

"Would you believe that this is my son, bubba?"

He looks at me incredulously for a moment before deciding on what to say.

"Sheeit, I reckon so. I know how you like to play with maggots in yer special area!" Lurch says with a big shit-eating grin plastered on his face.

"I do indeed, my friend. Lurch, this is Felch. Felch, this is Lurch! We are going to be one big, happy family."

"Howdy Felch!" Lurch beams.

"TeLl HiM hEllLo FrOm Me MoThEr!"

"Felch says hello!"

Felch then uses his halteres to lovingly stroke Lurch's head. It brings me so much joy to see this.

"He likes you already." I tell him.

"Well shucks, I like him too, I's guess, Miss Morticia!"

With introductions out of the way, Felch hungrily goes back to Kim's malformed corpse, excited to feed on her vile remains.

"How the fuck are you still alive, Lurch? I mean, I am totally stoked about it, but I watched Kim snuff your ass out good!"

"Well Miss Morticia, she did indeed kilt me. I died and went to Heaven and everythin'! I even got to see my sweet ole' Grandpappy again. And guess what? He could walk! After he kicked the bucket, he gots his feet back! Ain't that a stitch?"

"Wow! Did you find a trap door up there or something so you could sneak back, baby?"

"Well, Grandpappy showed me how to look down at yer loved ones on Earth, and I saw you were in heaps o' trouble and I knew I's had to come try to help you so I begged Grandpappy to help me come rescue you. He told me that God had granted him a wish if he shared his famous moonshine recipe on account that God must be a damn drunk or somethin'. And guess what, Miss Morticia? He gave me that wish cuz he ain't selfish! And I wished to be back with ya, but it teleported me back to the dad gummed Hurt 2 The Core facility. I had to hoof it all the way here. That's what took me so long!"

"How did you know to come to this house, though?" I asked.

"I dunno, it was likes I was plumb stuck, then's I's went's out yonder and I's see a blood trail and follower'd it to ya!"

"Thank goodness that God is a drunk piece of shit!" I say facetiously.

"Sheeit, don't make him take me back cuz of yer sass!" Lurch teases.

"So, what's next, ya think, Miss Morticia?"

"Well, a family needs a place to plant their roots like a tree and stick around. What do you say about the three of us heading up to Cowgill, Missouri, and staying at your Grandpappy's cabin?"

I watched the big man's chin tremble slightly as if he was fighting off a bad case of the cries. He quickly regained his jovial demeanor and beamed like a kid on picture day.

"That would tickle me pink! A real-life family. Who would've thunk it? "

"Well, what are we waiting for, then? Let us make like an egg and beat it."

We both must be on a mind meld as well, because we immediately hug one another for a very long time. It feels like home in the big dingus' arms. Okay, shoot me now, that sounds sappy as fuck! Quick, get me something to murder! After an unknown amount of time, we break from our heartfelt embrace. Lurch looks around the room; taking in the extreme amount of carnage everywhere with wide eyes. A heavy sigh escapes the big man when his eyes register the squashed body of a small child.

"This is wrong that Miss Kim could indercriminately kill youngins like this. I want us to pinkie-swear that we will never become somethin' like this one day. Somethin...' so... damn... Evil."

I survey the room and see the big guy's point. It looks like Kim had brought the lyric sheet from a Carcass album to life. The sheer amount of bodily mutilation was almost too much to take in at once. I looked down at the stomped and deflated dead child, drying brain matter had discharged out from every conceivable facial orifice. I felt a small tinge of despondency in my cold, black heart and could totally understand where Lurch was coming from with his immense sadness at all this destruction. He is a big softy after all.

"I promise, baby. We will never become crueler than we need to be. I never want to become as unhinged as Kim became. Maybe being the killing kind is not a way for me anymore. There comes a time in your life where you just must grow up and instead of destroying things, you want to create things instead."

"You really mean that, Miss Morticia? I's could never kill again and be pleased as punch about it!"

"Hell, yeah I mean it! Let us shake on it!"

Lurch puts out his baseball mitt-sized hand out for me to shake it. As I propel my hand towards his to reciprocate, I dip my hand into Kim's cunt clam chowder until it is caked in the creepy concoction and decisively shake his hand. Lurch gives me a pained look but smiles nonetheless at my continued depravity.

"This will be a cake-walk, Lurchy-poo. I could do this shit in my sleep; you just watch how much butt I can kick. More rumps than the entire Richard Laymon catalog combined!"

Chapter Twenty-Seven

Happily, Ever After?

SO, UHH, YEAH. THAT mindset lasted about five days; I think. I mean, I gave it a shot, did the old "college try" routine, but I just felt this massive black hole in the pit of my very being. I felt like a mere husk of my former self. I am Jack's absolute despondency. After the debacle at Judith's house was over, we made the long trek up to Cowgill, Missouri, formerly population 250, now 253!

Lurch's Grandpappy's cabin was still there and in fine shape, if I say so myself. It took some elbow grease from the three of us to get it in a livable condition after all those years of being abandoned. We even had to evict a rather unruly family of racoons that were vexed to have a bunch of humans show up at their home and boot them the fuck out! Sorry, not sorry!

After we got everything in order, I tried to walk the straight and narrow and block the delectable idea of carving up humans like cattle at a barbeque restaurant out of my morbid mind. I read tons of books by my favorite authors like Aron Beauregard, Judith Sonnet, Daniel J. Volpe, Peter Sotos and, especially Otis Bateman. I would go on long walks and just feel astonished that the closest home to us was over five miles away! My mind went to all the delicious possibilities when it came to human butchery.

Cowgill did not even have a police presence, for fuck's sake. The closest was in Polo, which was over seven miles away. I could probably murder every bumkin in this crappy town and no one would ever notice. Finally, I started digging a hole about 100 yards from the cabin. I would just go out there and start excavating. Lurch would help me out a lot, but it really confused him that I didn't know why I was doing it precisely. I just would laugh and tell him it was because I wanted to maintain my girlish figure.

Days turned into weeks, weeks turned into months, and I continued to dig. I felt like Fenton digging a dungeon in Frailty. Felch wanted to help but unfortunately he was useless, mostly due to a lack of hands and thumbs. I kissed his stubbly head and told him it was okay and just to go play. He happily buzzed off and fed on a dead opossum down by the creek. So, it was just me and Lurch being a couple of digging machines throughout the day. When we wanted to talk, we talked. When we wanted to eat, we ate.

At night, Lurch would build these amazing bonfires and the three of us would sing campfire songs or tell scary stories while we ate s'mores. We were a real family. It was something I must have yearned for subconsciously. I mean, it was something I had lacked my whole life. My "real family" was nothing more than a bunch of rabid weasels that tried to literally eat me alive. I was like a newborn in a crib with a bunch of starving sewer rats trying to devour me. I chose my new family with Lurch and made Felch in my very own womb.

For once in my life, I felt like I was a part of something. Tethered to something bigger than myself, if that makes any sense. Being here with my boys was easily the best part of my life. I even teared up a little by the firelight, the darkness helping me conceal my tears like a complicit accomplice. I did not want anyone seeing me be a sappy little bitch. I got a rep to protect you know!

It took another week of constant digging before I knew it was the right depth. I mean, I had no way to truly gauge this assessment. It was more of a gut feeling. Lurch and I were balls deep inside the pit digging away like that arcade game from the eighties, *Dig Dug*, when I cracked my back while stretching and tossed away my shovel like an unwanted thought.

"Dishes are done, man!" I said, mimicking Kenny Crandell from *Don't Tell Mom the Babysitter's Dead*.

"What dishes, Miss Morticia? All I sees is a buncha dirt!"

"It is just a line from a dumb movie, baby. It just means we are done, is all."

"Good, cuz my back is hurtin' me somethin' fierce. This was hard work! I still don't rightly know what fer, though."

But I knew. I guess I knew this whole damned time. I was digging this for the one thing I was truly good at. The one thing that made me feel alive, even though I was dead inside for the most part. It was preparation for the next phase of our lives in bum fuck Egypt. It was groundwork for my legacy.

"It is a giant body pit, baby. I am going to go back to doing my weekly murder streams. I have been getting bombarded to re-open my Only Fans from all of my past fanatics and a shitload of new ones from my stint at Hurt2The Core.com. This area is prime real estate for some truly barbaric butchery, don't you agree?"

"I reckon so." Lurch says cautiously.

"Everyone from H2TC is dead and gone, my friend, Lux included. No one is going to come look for us, I promise. It will be good money that we will need. That way, we can be lazy fuckers the rest of the time and just enjoy life. I might even give writing a shot. Who knows, maybe there are a bunch of weirdos out there that might enjoy my gore whore antics and eat up my stories like a cannibal at the paraplegic wing in a hospital."

Chapter Twenty-Eight

A New Beginning

THE DAY WAS AS brilliant as a perfectly polished diamond wedding ring. I just finished recording the newest installment of "Morticia's Macabre Theatre". Sounds awesome, right? Lurch is carrying out what little remains of the pederast rapist that I just bisected piece by piece, slower than molasses, by the way, to toss it into our pit tomb. His wretched screams had kept the boys up most of the night, which caused them to be pissy at me all morning long. I tried to cheer them up by cooking them both a big breakfast, and unlike the Ice Cube song, I cooked it with hog, cuz swine is fine in my book! After everyone filled their bellies, we strolled outside to enjoy the day together as a family. Felch buzzed around me incessantly with palpable excitement.

"MoThEr, MaY I pLeAsE pLaY iN tHe GrAvE pIt?"

"Of course, son, go have some fun." I tell him and kiss him gently on his bulbous head.

He makes a beeline for the body pit and dives into the gelatinous, malodorous ooze like an Olympic diver with a splash. The fermenting, rotting bodies have made a sea of stinking and sludgy slop, a river of revolting rot, if you will. Countless insects and maggots writhe on the surface, feasting on the festering scabs and infected human facial tissue and other assorted amputated limbs that I have ravaged, torn, and punctured. All the carcass's ooze from multiple stab or cutting wounds. The dermis weeps pus from the avulsed and sliced wounds. Clear, viscous fluids are purged from the hacks and disgorgement of the deteriorated, mis-shapen corpses. The whole thing reeks of putrefaction, but like most things in this shitty world, you can get used to anything if you set your mind to it.

I set two beach chairs up close to the corpse pit. Lurch gets in his and stretches out comfortably while I shimmy out of my clothes so that I am as nude as the day I was born. The rays from the sun warm my body, causing me to become heavily aroused. The balminess causes my nipples to stiffen and makes me tweak my teat and cup my breasts seductively. I feel a warmth cascading from between my legs, immersing my pubic hair in my fluids. Lurch blushes from my rampant horniness, but he should be used to my shenanigans by now.

A human femur bone lays besides my chair. I pick it up and stroke my clitoris with it. I lightly tease my pussy as I rub the bone between my folds, drenching me even more than I was previously. I slowly push the bone inside of me and hiss in pleasure like a steaming pipe. It goes in easier than a hot knife in butter. I edge myself towards orgasmic bliss a few times before I am primed up for the real deal, as this was merely foreplay. I pull out the bone from my hungry pussy with a popping suctioning sound. Cunny juice tethers my scorching box with the bone momentarily before I toss it to the ground beside my chair with a clatter.

"I think I am going to go for a dip, baby." I tell Lurch in a husky voice that I can barely recognize.

"Sounds good, Miss Morticia! Now don't be stayin' in that crud too long or else you mights get pretty sick!"

"I doubt I can get sicker than I already am, bubba. You already know that I am a certifiable nut job."

" Don'ts I knows it!"

I blow him a kiss and dip my toe into the meaty miasma and playfully kick it up into the air, speckling me with the flavorful gore. I wade into the mucus, phlegm and bile and revel in debauched disgust mixed with eroticism. I wade further into the sanguine guts, septic vomit, and putrid offal and squeal in delight as I feel the meaty marinara tickle my anal cavity and submerge my pussy in its fetid odors. I spread my labia lips apart as wide as possible and use the cup of my palm as a kind of bowl so I can stuff myself with the odious, reeking gruel. Detached ulcers engulfed with maggots and vermin, smothered with gastric juices, all get crammed in my quavering clam, sending wave upon wave of orgasms throughout my body.

I take my hands and dive them into the gore, retrieving fistfuls of infected and moldering flesh, caking my titties with hot, bubbling, molten gristle and fermenting innards that are heavily decomposed. I take great handfuls and slurp up the concoction and eat the decay like a scrumptious meal. I dive under the sea of liquified and minced carcasses and swim in its vile essence, reveling in this revolting form of self-degradation.

I break through the surface of vile viscera like a shark's dorsal fin totally encased in blood, pus, and gastric juices. My body is a burgundy hue, making me resemble someone who was beaten to death with a bat. I spit out a mouthful of maggots and drowned cockroaches in to the air like a nightmarish version of a water fountain.

I turn to see Felch hungrily lapping up the putrid erupted pustules, moist flesh packed in pancreatic juices and what looks like a partially ingested decomposing brain. I read his thoughts. He is in heaven, and is radiating nothing but glee. I look over at Lurch, who is now over at the creek fishing and whistling a jaunty tune, obviously recalling a fond memory of himself and his dear old grandpappy. He looks over at me and gives me an ecstatic wave. I do not have to be a psychic or mind-meld with the big, fruit loop dingus to know that he is happy as a pig in shit. As for me, I am living my best life. I am with my two favorite people and I get to kill as many douchebags as I please, to the joy of all my adoring and blood-thirsty fans all over the internet.

I also get to indulge in my filthy fetish of turning myself into a human septic tank with my putrid pool of human rot and decay. I guess you can say that in the end, I got everything I wanted. I got a great life, a great best friend, a great kid, and a great home. I got to keep my dream job, and I get to do whatever makes me happy. I won. I beat Kim White and every other obstacle that has been thrown in my way. They did not destroy me. I destroyed them. I persevered. And for that I am Jack's smirking revenge.

Afterword

Wow, what a fantastic, stressful ride this has been! It seems totally surreal that I am sitting here writing a freaking afterward for Maggot Girl part 3! I just tabulated the total word count for all three episodes and we are sitting at roughly 85,684 filthy words! Pure lunacy, right? Who the hell would have thought I would get any readers, let alone garner any kind of following??? (Maggot Colony, I am looking at you!) the Extreme horror community is filled with countless wonderful and crazy individuals! Give yourselves a round of applause! Below, you will find the condescend version of how this gross little story came to fruition. It is nothing mind-blowing, but it is a fun little story in and of itself! Enjoy!

   The creation of Maggot Girl initially began as SC Mendes of Bloodbound Books fame and I were trying to get ahold of the infamous blog writer of the notorious "*Blowfly Girl*" blog. It was, in essence, about an abhorrent young girl that would fill her vagina full of rotten meat and maggots, and then got deathly sick. Hmm, that sounds strangely familiar, right? Well, we managed to get ahold of them through email, but they ended up being extremely "flaky." They said we could use the journal entries to form a loose manuscript, and did not want any form of compensation or recognition for it. But at the end of the day, things just did not pan out for this project. The idea of the story kept gestating in my little pea brain and would not go away, though. I mean, if the writings were true, what kind of individual would get off on such a dangerous and deplorable fetish?

Well, being a nutjub such as myself, I thought like most writers do; I wondered *what doing something like that would feel like*. Or better yet, what was their mindset, and what would it do to them physically? Of course, I tumbled down a rabbit hole of perversity, and much like our beloved maggot maiden herself, I dived right the fuck in and never looked back. I initially set out to write the original author's blog entries into a narrative structure, but quickly realized there was not much material to go very far with it. Besides, I wanted a more fantastical take on the subject, even though the story was quite heinous to begin with. I also wanted my first foray into extreme horror to pack a wallop and to leave a lasting impression with readers, in case I was a "one and done" type of writer.

I mean, Maggot Girl episode 1 might not even make a blip on the radar in the extreme horror sub-genre. I had no idea what the reception would be and, more importantly, I felt like a tourist; a faker. What business did I even have trying to be a writer in the extreme horror/ Splatterpunk genre? I mean the nerve of some people, right??? I luckily landed two very helpful authors who initially give me a lot of help, guidance and verve. Regina Watts and Simon McHardy, I am looking at you! I am your guys' fault!

I set out making my take on a Euro Guro manga, paying homage to my favorite artist, Uziga Waita, creator of the blasphemous *Mai Chan's Daily Life*, among countless other artistic atrocities. I love how batshit crazy this manga are; they revel in absolute butchery and sexual depravity. So, I of course set out to make a literary guro book, chock full of crazy gross sex and disgusting violence. With bated breath, I submitted the story, a mere 37 pages, but boy oh boy, those pages were filled with the nastiest shit I could imagine. It did not take long till I started to receive feedback, mostly good to boot! I felt encouraged to continue. Even though I did not "blow up," the story seemed popular amongst the more die-hard extreme horror fans, and the people that read it truly liked it. I also kind of liked how Maggot Girl was there to shock some clueless reader that happened upon it. A true underground type of book, a fitting place for maggots, right? Once I got a taste of people wanting more Morticia, I was amped up to start episode 2. My goal was to make it bigger and better in every way. More gore, more characters, more pages! I was all ready to start, and that is when my life torpedoed out of control, causing me not to write for over seven months.

What had happened, without getting too much into it, was basically me and my wife separated for a time, causing me to fall into a deep depression. What little I wrote, I absolutely hated with a passion. Episode 2 went through many stages before the final version came out via godless. I had around 10K written and I scrapped it all. I was very angry during that time and it showed in the manuscript. Even though Maggot Girl is totally disgusting, I still like to keep a fun air about things. Morticia cracking jokes, fun references etc. this version had none of it. All work and no play made Morticia a dull girl. It was not authentic to the past writing at all. It was all cynicism, mean-spiritedness, and unrestrained carnage cranked to eleven!

Well, luckily for me, my wife took me back, and we worked on our marriage, making it stronger in the process. Yay for us! In my spare time at night, I would write. My full-time job impeded the process. I am a blue-collar worker, so the work is very physical, causing me to be lazy after long shifts sometimes. I pushed forward anyway, and slowly Morticia's real voice came back and the writing flourished once again. I had always been fascinated with snuff films and Redrooms, so I knew that was an element I wanted to incorporate for part 2. I also wanted Morticia to have a sidekick. *Of Mice and Men* is a favorite book of mine and I wanted her partner to be like Lenny Small from the John Steinbeck classic. But this story was going to be extreme so a part of me thought what if I also incorporate Ed Lee's Bighead character as well since that is another favorite. Thus, Lurch Beauregard was born! Yes, I named him after a horror hero of mine, Aron Beauregard. I also dedicated Episode 3 to him, as well as Judith Sonnet, who appears in episode 3 as a very pivotal character. They both are class acts and I am a huge fan of both of them.

The final addition was my Patrick Bateman character, Pat Bale. I wanted a character that was truly evil, and I think some of his passages are downright blasphemous. I even tried to restrain his passages and antics. The first version of his deeds was way too horrible if you can believe it, LOL. I am proud of that depraved bastard! I truly think Episode 2 is one of the most depraved books out there, but I am biased! Read it and see if you have not yet.

Part 3 is special to me. I took some daring and bold moves with the story line. A true third entry type of decision, it seems. I fully admit to doing some wacky shit with this one! I also wanted to test the waters and see if I could achieve something other than revulsion with the story. I tried to create some heartfelt scenes; dare I say, try to generate a genuine tearjerker moment or two. Only you, dear reader, can tell me if I achieved that or not. I cried, but I am a softie and these are my babies.

I initially thought that I was going somewhat lax during the first half of the story in terms of gore, and I worried I did not make the finale hardcore enough. And then we get up to the home invasion part of the book and Kim really stepped it up in that department! I think I exceeded my expectations in terms of gore from then till the end of the book. I am especially proud of the gross shit I came up with for the "body pit pool sequence." I did try to limit the excessive Easter eggs in the final chapter, as my editor, the wonderful Candace Nola, suggested. I kept the brilliant "I am Jack's" though, I say those in real life all the time and it still felt integral to Morticia's dialogue. I do not think Chuck Palahniuk will mind, and if he does, I know a particular gruesome twosome that might make him the star of a very popular, very brutal online slaughter special called Morticia's Macabre Theatre!

Thanks for sticking around and listening to this long-winded explanation on how this series came to be. It was a hell of a run, but all good things must come to an end. Besides, if enough people want it, I am sure I could come up with a new story down the road for our demented duo and Felch. I left it in a good place to pick back up one day, Don't cha reckon?

But for now, I am excited to explore new books and create new stories and characters, and weave some more worlds. One thing I can promise is that I will always push the boundaries of horror as much as possible while still trying to tell a great story! Thanks to all who like my stuff and have given me a voice. You guys keep reading them, and I will keep writing them!

Printed in Great Britain
by Amazon